REBEL SPURS

REBEL

 # SPURS

ANDRE NORTON

THE WORLD PUBLISHING COMPANY

CLEVELAND AND NEW YORK

Published by The World Publishing Company
2231 West 110th Street, Cleveland 2, Ohio

Published simultaneously in Canada by
Nelson, Foster & Scott Ltd.

Library of Congress Catalog Card Number: 62-13944

Second Printing

2WP663

For HENDRY PEART
and CARROLL COLLINS
*who share my interest
in "The West."*

1 ❋

EVEN THE COMING of an autumn dusk could not subdue the color of this land. Shadows here were not gray or black; they were violet and purple. The crumbling adobe walls were laced by strings of crimson peppers, vivid in the torch and lantern light. It had been this way for days, red and yellow, violet—colors he had hardly been aware existed back in the cool green, silver, gray-brown of Kentucky.

So this was Tubacca! The rider shifted his weight in the saddle and gazed about him with watchful interest. Back in '59 this had been a flourishing town, well on its way to prominence in the Southwest. The mines in the hills behind producing wealth, the fact that it was a watering place on two cross-country routes—the one from Tucson down into Sonora of Old Mexico, the other into California—had all fed its growth.

Then the war . . . The withdrawal of the army, the invasion of Sibley's Confederate forces which had reached this far in the persons of Howard's Arizona Rangers—and most of all the raiding, vicious, deadly, and continual, by Apaches and outlaws—had blasted Tubacca. Now, in the fall of 1866, it was a third of what it had been, with a ragged fringe of dilapidated adobes crumbling back into the soil. Only this heart core was still alive in the dusk.

Smell, a myriad of smells, some to tickle a flat stomach, others to wrinkle the nose. Under the rider the big stud moved, tossed his head, drawing the young man's attention from the town back to his own immediate concerns. The animal he rode, the two he led were, at first glance, far more noticeable than the dusty rider himself.

His saddle was cinched about the barrel of a big gray colt, one that could not have been more than five years old but showed enough power and breeding to attract attention in any horse-conscious community. Here was a thorough-bred of the same blood which had pounded race tracks in Virginia and in Kentucky to best all comers. Even now, after weeks on the trail, with a day's burden of alkali dust grimed into his coat, the stud was a beautiful thing. And his match was the mare on the lead rope, plainly a lady of family, perhaps of the same line, since her coat was also silver. She crowded closer, nickered plaintively.

She was answered by an anxious bray from the fourth member of the party. The mule bearing the trail pack was in ludicrous contrast to his own aristocratic companions. His long head, with one entirely limp and flopping ear, was grotesquely ugly, the carcass beneath the pack a bone rack, all sharp angles and dusty hide. Looks, however, as his master could have proven, were deceiving.

"Soooo—" The rider's voice was husky from swallowing trail grit, but it was tuned to the soothing croon of a practiced horse trainer. "Sooo—lady, just a little farther now, girl . . ."

From the one-story building on the rider's right a man emerged. He paused to light a long Mexican cigarillo, and as he held the match to let the sulfur burn away, his eyes fell upon the stallion. A casual interest tightened into open appreciation as he stepped from under the porch-overhang into the street.

"That is some horse, sir." His voice was that of an educated gentleman. The lantern at the end of the porch picked out the fine ruffled linen of his shirt, a vest with a painted design of fighting cocks, and the wink of gold buttons. The rather extravagant color of his clothing matched well with the town.

"I think so." The answer was short and yet not discourteous.

Again the mare voiced her complaint, and the rider turned to the gentleman. "There is a livery stable here, suh?" Unconsciously he reverted in turn to the rather formal speech pattern of another place and time.

The man in the painted vest had transferred his attention from stallion to mare. "Yes. Quickest way is down this alley. Tobe Kells owns it. He's a tolerable vet, too. She's near her time, ain't she?"

"Yes." The rider raised one finger to the straight wide brim of his low-crowned black hat. He was already turning his mount when the townsman added:

"No hotel here, stranger. But the Four Jacks serves a pretty good meal and keeps a couple of beds for overnighters. You're welcome back when you've settled the little lady. She Virginia stock?"

"Kentucky," the rider answered, and then his lips tightened into a compressed line. Was it a mistake to admit even that much? He would have to watch every word he said in this town. He tugged gently at the lead rope and walked Shiloh ahead at a pace which did not urge Shadow to any great effort. The mule, Croaker, fell in behind her so that they were strung out in the familiar pattern which had been theirs clear from Texas.

Minutes later her owner was rubbing down the fretful Shadow, murmuring the soothing words to quiet her. The lean, gray-haired man who had ushered them into the stable stood eyeing the mare's distended sides.

"I'd say, young fellow, you didn't git her here a mite too soon, no, siree. She's due right quick. Carryin' a blood foal, I'm thinkin'—"

"Yes. How soon? Tonight?"

Tobe Kells made a quick examination. The mare, after a first nervous start, stood easy under his sure and gentle hands. "Late, maybe. First foal?"

"Yes." Her owner hesitated and then added, "You give me a hand with her?"

"You bet, son. She's a pretty thing, an' she's been a far piece, I'd say. Now you looky here, boy—you sure look like you could take some curryin' an' corn fodder under your belt too. You git over to th' Four Jacks. Topham's got him a Chinee cookin' there who serves up th' best danged grub in this here town. Fill up your belly an' take some ease. Then if we do have this little lady gittin' us up tonight, you'll be ready for it. I'll see t' th' stud an' th' mule. That colt's not a wild one." Kells surveyed Shiloh knowingly. "No, I seed he was gentle-trained when you come in." He ran his hand down Shiloh's shoulder, touched the brand. "Spur R? That ain't no outfit I heard tell of before."

"From Eastern . . . Texas—" That much was true. All three animals had been given the brand in the small Texas town where the wagon train had assembled. And perhaps this was the time when he should begin building up the background one Drew Kirby must present to Tubacca, Arizona Territory. "All right, I'll go eat." He picked up his saddlebags. "You'll call me if——"

"Sure, son. Say, I don't rightly know your name. . . ."

"Drew Kirby."

"Wal, sure, Kirby, Tobe Kells is a man o' his word. Iffen there's any reason to think you'll be needed, I'll send Callie along for you. Callie!"

At Kells' hail a boy swung down the loft ladder. He was wiry thin, with a thick mop of sun-bleached hair and a flashing grin. At the sight of Shiloh and Shadow he whistled.

"Now ain't they th' purtiest things?" he inquired of the stable at large. " 'Bout th' best stock we've had here since th' last time *Don* Cazar brought in a couple o' hissen. Where'll I put your plunder, mister?" He was already loosing Croaker's pack. "You be stayin' over to th' Jacks?"

Drew glanced up at the haymow from which Callie had just descended. "Any reason why I can't bunk up there?" he asked Kells.

"None 'tall, Kirby, none 'tall. Know you want to be handy like. Stow that there gear up above, Callie, an' don't you drop nothin'. Rest yourself easy, son. These here hosses is goin' to be treated jus' like th' good stuff they is."

"Croaker, also." Drew stopped by the mule, patted the long nose, gave a flip to the limp ear. "He's good stuff, too— served in the cavalry . . ."

Kells studied the young man by the mule. Cavalry saddle on the stud, two Colt pistols belted high and butt forward, and that military cord on his hat—army boots, too. The liveryman knew the signs. This was not the first veteran to drift into Tubacca; he wouldn't be the last either. Seems

like half of both them armies back east didn't want to go
home an' sit down peaceful like now that they was through
wi' shootin' at each other. No, siree, a right big herd o' 'em
was trailin' out here. An' he thought he could put name to
the color of coat this young'un had had on his back, too.
Only askin' more than a man volunteered to tell, that warn't
neither manners nor wise.

"He gits th' best, too, Kirby." Kells shifted a well-chewed
tobacco cud from one cheek to the other.

He could trust Kells, Drew thought. A little of his concern over Shadow eased. He shouldered the saddlebags and
made his way back down the alley, beginning to see the
merit in the liveryman's suggestions. Food—and a bath!
What he wouldn't give for a bath! Hay to sleep on was
fine; he had had far worse beds during the past four years.
But a hot bath to be followed by a meal which was not the
jerky, corn meal, bitter coffee of trail cooking! His pace
quickened into a trot but slackened again as he neared the
Four Jacks and remembered all the precautions he must
take in Tubacca.

In the big room of the cantina oil lamps made yellow
pools of light. The man in the painted vest was seated at a
table laying out cards in a complicated pattern of a solitaire
game. And at one side a round-faced Mexican in ornate,
south-of-the-border clothing held a guitar across one plump
knee, now and then plucking absent-mindedly at a single
string as he stared raptly into space. A third man stood
behind the bar polishing thick glasses.

"Greetings!" As Drew stood blinking just within the
doorway the card player rose. He was a tall, wide-shouldered
man, a little too thin for his height. Deep lines in his clean-
shaven face bracketed his wide mouth. His curly hair was a

silvery blond, and he had dark, deeply set eyes. "I'm Reese Topham, owner of this oasis," he introduced himself.

"Drew Kirby." He must remember that always—he was Drew Kirby, a Texan schooled with kinfolk in Kentucky, who served in the war under Forrest and was now drifting west, as were countless other rootless Confederate veterans. Actually the story was close enough to the truth. And he had had months on the trail from San Antonio to Santa Fe, then on to Tucson, to study up on any small invented details. He was Drew Kirby, Texan, not Drew Rennie of Red Springs, Kentucky.

"For a man just off the trail, Kirby, the Four Jacks does have a few of the delights of civilization. A bath . . ." One of Topham's dark eyebrows, so in contrast to his silvery hair, slid up inquiringly, and he grinned at Drew's involuntary but emphatic nod. "One of nature's gifts to our fair city is the hot spring. Hamilcar!" His hand met table top in a sharp slap. The Mexican jerked fully awake and looked around. From the back of the cantina emerged a middle-aged Negro.

"Yes, Mistuh Reese, suh?"

"Customer for you, Hamilcar. I would judge he wants the full treatment. This, Mister Kirby, is the best barber, valet, and general aid to comfort in town, the sultan of our bath. Hamilcar, Mister Kirby would like to remove the layers of dust he has managed to pick up. Good luck to you both!"

Drew found himself laughing as he followed Hamilcar to the rear of the building.

Topham had reason to be proud of his bath, Drew admitted some time later. A natural hot spring might be the base of the luxury, but man's labor had piped the water into stone-slab tubs and provided soap and towels. To sit and soak was a delight he had forgotten. He shampooed his unkempt head vigorously and allowed himself to forget all worries, wallowing in the sheer joy of being really clean again.

Hamilcar had produced a clean shirt and drawers from the saddlebags, even managing to work up a shadow of shine on the scuffed cavalry boots, and had beat the worst of the trail dust from the rest of the traveler's clothing. Drew had re-dressed except for his gun belt when he heard a voice call from the next cubicle.

"Ham—Ham! You git yourself in here, 'fore I skin that black hide—"

"Johnny!" Topham's voice cut through the other's thickened slur. "You soak that rot-gut out of you, and mind your tongue while you do it!"

"Sure, sure, Reese—" The voice was pitched lower this time, but to Drew the tone was more mocking than conciliatory. Drunk or sober, that stranger did not hold very kindly thoughts of Topham. But that was none of the Kentuckian's business.

"Yore hat, suh." Hamilcar brought in the well-brushed headgear, much more respectable looking than it had been an hour ago. The cord on it glistened. Army issue—brave gold bullion—made for a general's wearing. Drew straightened it, remembering . . .

Sergeant Rennie of the Scouts, in from an independent foray into enemy-held Tennessee, reporting to the Old Man himself—General Bedford Forrest. And Forrest saying:

"We don't give medals, Sergeant. But I think a good soldier might just be granted a birthday present without any one gittin' too excited about how military that is." Then he had jerked the cord off his own hat and given it to Drew. It was something big to remember when you were only nineteen and had been soldiering three years, three years with a dogged army that refused to be beaten. That hat cord, the spurs on his boots, they were all he had brought home from war—save a tough body and a mind he hoped was as hard.

"Mighty pretty hat trimmin', that, suh," Hamilcar admired.

"Mighty big man wore it once." Drew was still half in the past. "What do I owe you more'n the thanks of a mighty tired man you've turned out brand new again?" He smiled and was suddenly all boy.

"Foah bits, suh. An' it was a pleasure to do fo' a gentleman. It truly was. Come agin, suh—come, agin!"

Drew went down the corridor, his spurs answering with a chiming ring each time his heels met planking. Worn at Chapultepec by a Mexican officer, they had been claimed as spoils of war in '47 by a Texas Ranger. And in '61 the Ranger's son, Anson Kirby, had jingled off in them to another war. Then Kirby had disappeared during that last scout in Tennessee, vanishing into nowhere when he fell wounded from the saddle, smashing into a bushwhackers' hideout.

On a Sunday in May of '65, back in Gainesville, when Forrest's men had finally accepted surrender and the deadness of defeat, a Union trooper had worn those spurs into church. And Boyd Barrett had sold his horse the same day to buy back those silver bits because he knew what they meant to his cousin Drew. Now here Drew was, half the continent away from Gainesville and Tennessee, wearing

Anse's spurs and half of Anse's name—to find a father he had not known was still alive, until last year.

The Kentuckian was sure of only one thing right now, he was not going to enter a town or a stretch of country where Hunt Rennie was *the* big man, and claim to be Rennie's unknown son. Maybe later he could come to a decision about his action. But first he wanted to be sure. There might well be no place for a Drew Rennie in Hunt Rennie's present life. They were total strangers and perhaps it must be left that way.

There was no reason for him to claim the kinship. He was independent. Drew Kirby had a mule and two good horses, maybe three by tomorrow. Aunt Marianna had insisted that he accept part of the Mattock estate, even though his Kentucky grandfather had left him penniless. He'd made his choice without hesitation: the colt Shiloh, the mare Shadow, and she bred to Storm Cloud for what should be a prize foal. His aunt had made him take more—gold in his money belt, enough to give him a start in the west. He was his own man, not Rennie's son, unless he chose . . .

Two more lamps had been lighted in the cantina. Drew sat down at a table. There was a swish of full skirts, and he looked up at a girl. She smiled as if she liked what she saw of this brown-faced stranger with quiet, disciplined features and eyes older than his years.

"You like, *señor* . . tequila . . . whiskee . . . food?"

"Food, *señorita*. You see a most hungry man."

She laughed and then frowned anxiously. "Ah, but, *señor,* this is a time when the cupboard is, as you would say, bare! When the wagons come—then what a difference! Now, tortillas, frijoles, maybe some fruit . . . sweet for the tongue, like wine in the throat. Perhaps an egg—"

"To me that is a feast." Drew fell into the formal speech which seemed natural here. "You see one who has done his own trail cooking too long."

"Ah—*el pobrete*—poor man! Surely there will be an egg!" She was gone and Drew began covertly to study the other men in the room.

In any western town the cantina, or saloon, was the meeting place for masculine society. Even if Hunt Rennie did not appear bodily in the Four Jacks tonight, Drew could pick up information about his father merely by keeping open ears. As far away as Santa Fe he had heard of Rennie's Range and *Don* Cazar (the name the Mexicans had given its owner, Hunt Rennie).

Escaped from a Mexican prison in 1847, believing his wife and the son he had never seen to be dead, Hunt Rennie had gone west. In contrast to the tragedy of his personal life, whatever Rennie had turned his hand to in the new territory had prospered. A prospector he had grub-staked, found the Oro Cruz, one of the richest mines in the Tubacca hills. Rennie owned two freighting lines, one carrying goods to California, the other up from Sonora. And his headquarters in the fertile Santa Cruz Valley was a ranch which was also a fort, a fort even the Apaches avoided after they had suffered two overwhelming defeats there.

That was Rennie's Range—cultivated fields, fruit orchards, *manadas* of fine horses. *Don* Cazar supplied Tucson and the army posts with vegetables and superb hams. He had organized a matchless company of Pima Indian Scouts after the army pulled out in '61, had fought Apaches, but had sided with neither Union nor Confederate forces. During the war years he had more or less withdrawn within the borders of the Range, offering refuge to settlers and miners fleeing

Indian attacks. *Don* Cazar was a legend now, and a man did not quickly claim kinship with a legend.

"Want a room, Kirby?" Topham paused beside his table.

"No. I have to stay close to the mare."

"Yes. I can understand that. Kells is good with horses, so you needn't worry. Ever raced that colt of yours?"

"Not officially." Drew smiled. There was that lieutenant with the supply wagons. The man hadn't talked so loudly about Johnny Rebs after Shiloh showed his heels to the roan the soldiers had bragged up.

"This is a sporting town when the wagons come in, and they're due tomorrow. Johnny Shannon just rode in to report. Might be some racing. You aim to stay on in Tubacca?"

"Have to until Shadow can trail again. How's the prospect for a job?"

"With cattle—horses—teaming?"

"Horses, I guess."

"Well, *Don* Cazar—Rennie—runs the best *manadas*. You might hit him for work. He'll be riding in to meet the wagons. Carmencita, did you bring all that was left of the supplies?" Topham's quizzical eyebrows lifted in greeting to the waitress's loaded tray. "I'd say, young man, that you are facing a full-time job now, getting all that inside of you."

Drew ate steadily, consuming eggs and beans, tortillas, and fruit. Topham joined three men at the next table, substantial town citizens, Drew judged. The owner of the cantina raised his glass.

"Gentlemen, I give you another successful trading trip!"

"Saw Johnny ride in," one of the men returned. "Kid seems to be settlin' down, ain't he? That ought to be good news for Rennie."

"One believes in reformations when they are proven by time, *Señor* Cahill," the man wearing rich but somber Spanish clothing replied.

"It sure must go hard with a man to have his son turn out a wild one," commented the third.

Drew's cup was at his lips, but he did not drink. Whose son? Rennie's?

"No son by blood, that much comfort *Don* Cazar has. But foster ties are also strong. And the boy is still very young—"

"A rattler with only one button on the tail carries as much poison as a ten-button one. Rennie ought to cut losses and give that kid the boot. The way he's going he could involve Hunt in a real mess," Cahill said.

"You are *Don* Cazar's good friend, *Don* Reese, his *compadre* of many years. Can you not do something?"

"*Don* Lorenzo, all men have blind spots. And Johnny Shannon is Rennie's. Bob Shannon helped free Hunt out of Mex prison in the war and was killed doing it. Soon as Hunt set up here he sent for the boy and tried to give him a father."

"It is a great pity he has no child of his own blood. I have seen him stand here in Tubacca giving toys and candy to the little ones. Yet he has only this wild one under his roof, and perhaps that Juanito will break his heart in the end. . . ."

Drew put down his cup. It was very hard not to turn and ask questions. Dropping some coins on the table, he rose and started back to the stable, to the world of Shiloh and Shadow where he was unable to betray Drew Rennie. But there was so much Drew Kirby must learn—and soon!

2 ✳

Two LIGHTED LANTERNS hung from pegs along the center of the stable, and Callie had mounted a barrel to put up a third as Drew entered. There were the soft peaceful sounds of horses crunching fodder, hoofs rustling in straw. Shadow turned her head and nickered as Drew came up to her box stall. She was answered by a blowing from Shiloh, a bray out of Croaker.

"It's all right, girl—pretty lady—" Drew fondled her mane, stroked the satin-smooth arch of neck. Callie dropped from his barrel perch.

"She sure is right purty, Mister Kirby. Mister Kells said as to tell you he's sleepin' on a cot in th' tack room over there, should you be needin' him." Callie pointed. "Me, I'm beddin' down in the last stall. I put your gear up right over here, so's you can hear if she gits to movin'—"

"Thanks." Drew felt in a pocket, tossed Callie the coin his fingers found.

The boy caught the piece, his eyes round as he looked at it. "Lordy! Thanks, Mister Kirby! You must be near as shiny as *Don* Cazar—or Mister Topham!"

"Shiny?"

Callie laughed. "Silver-shiny! Ain't too many men as goes round Tubacca throwin' out good money thataway. 'Less it's ringin' down on th' bar, or slidin' 'cross some table 'cause they found out as how they was holdin' Jacks against some other fella's Kings. You want anything—you jus' holler, Mister Kirby!"

"Mister?" Drew thought he did not have the advantage of Callie by more than four or five years.

"Oh—Captain Kirby, maybe? Or Lieutenant? Johnny Shannon—now he was a lieutenant with Howard's Rangers." Callie gave Drew a shrewd measuring look.

"Sergeant." Drew corrected automatically and then asked: "How did you know I'd been in the army?"

"Well, you wear them two shootin' irons army style, belted high an' butt to front. Must use a flip-hand draw as do all th' hoss soldiers. Listen, Mister Kirby, iffen you rode with th' Rebs, you better keep your lip buttoned up when th' Blue Bellies hit town. There's been a pile of fightin' an' folks is gittin' mad 'bout it—"

"Blue Bellies?" Drew was wrenched back months, a year, by that old army slang. "Union troops stationed here?" He had unconsciously tensed, his body responding nerve and muscle to past training and alarms. But there were no Yanks or Rebs any more, no riders or marchers in blue and gray— just United States troops.

"There's a garrison out to the Mesa camp. An' Cap'n Bayliss, he don't take kindly to Rebs. You see, it's this way. . . . Out in th' breaks there's a bunch of Rebs—leastways they claim as how they's Rebs—still holdin' out. They hit an' run, raidin' ranches an' mines; they held up a coach a while back. An' so far they've ridden rings round th' cap'n. Now he thinks as how any Reb blowin' in town could be one of 'em, comin' to sniff out some good pickin's. So anyone as can't explain hisself proper to th' cap'n gits locked up out at camp till he can—"

"Trifle highhanded, ain't he?"

"Well, th' cap'n's for law an' order, an' he's army. But folks ain't likin' it too much. So far he's been doin' it though."

Drew frowned. So even this far away from the scene of old battles the war still smoldered; the black bitterness of defeat was made harder by the victor. Drew's hand rubbed across the bulge beneath his shirt. In one pocket of the money belt were his papers, among them the parole written out in Gainesville which could prove he had ridden with General Forrest's command, far removed from any Arizona guerrilla force. But to produce that would change Drew Kirby to Drew Rennie, and that he did not want to do.

"I rode with General Forrest, attached to General Buford's Scouts," he said absently.

"General Forrest!" Callie glowed. "Lordy, Mister Kirby, that's sure somethin', it sure is! Only don't be sayin' that round Cap'n Bayliss neither. He has him a big hate for General Forrest—seems like Bayliss was a colonel once till th' General outsmarted him back east. An' there was a big smoke-up 'bout it. They cut th' cap'n's spurs for him, an' he ended th' war out here. Now he ain't no patient man; he's th' kind as uses his hooks hard when he's ridin'.

"You know, you sure can tell a lot 'bout a man when you give a look at his hoss after he's come off th' trail. That there Shiloh colt o' yours, an' this here lady hoss, an' that old mule . . . anyone can see as how they's always been handled nice an' easy. They ain't got no spite 'gainst nobody as wants to rub 'em down an' give 'em a feed. But some hosses what git brung in here—they's white-eyed an' randy, does you give 'em a straight stare. For that there's always a reason. Mostly you can see what it is when you look good an' steady at th' men who was ridin' 'em!"

Drew laughed. "Glad I passed your test, Callie. Guess I'll turn in now. Been a long day travelin'—"

"Sure thing. An' from up there you can hear this little old mare, does she need you."

The Kentuckian's pack had been hoisted into the mow, and Callie had even humped up the fragrant hay to mattress his bedroll. A window was open to the night, and as Drew stretched out wearily, he could hear the distant tinkle of a guitar, perhaps from the Four Jacks. Somewhere a woman began to sing, and the liquid Spanish words lulled him asleep.

He roused suddenly, his hand flashing under his head before he returned to full consciousness, fingers tightening on the Colt he had placed there. Not the mare—no—rather the pound of running feet and then a cry . . .

"No, *señor*, no! *No es verdad*—it is not true! Teodoro, he meant no harm—!"

Drew scrambled to the window. Out in the alley below, three figures reeled in the circle of light afforded by the door lantern. The Kentuckian marked the upward swing of a quirt lash, saw a smaller shape fling up an arm in a vain attempt to ward off the blow. Another, the one who cried out, was belaboring the flogger with empty fists, and the voice was that of a girl!

To slide down the loft ladder was again nearer instinct than planned action. Shiloh snorted as Drew's boots rapped on the stable floor. The Kentuckian had no idea of the rea-

son for that fight, but he ran out with the vague notion that
an impartial referee was needed.

"You there—what's goin' on!" Sergeant Rennie came to
life again in the snapped demand.

The one who fled the quirt came up against the side of
the building almost shoulder to shoulder with Drew. And
he was only a boy, about Callie's age, his black hair flopping over eyes wide with shock and fright. Drew's hand
moved, and the lantern light glinted plainly on the barrel
of the Colt. For a moment they were all still as if sight of
the weapon had frozen them.

The attacker faced Drew directly. He was young and
handsome, if you discounted a darkening bruise already
puffing under one eye, a lip cut and swelling, a scowl twist-
ing rather heavy brows and making an ugly square of his
mistreated mouth.

"An' who th' devil are you?"

His voice was thick and slurred. Drew guessed that he
had not only been in a fight but that he was partly drunk.
Yet, as he faced the stranger eye to eye, the Kentuckian was
as wary as he had been when bellying down a Tennessee
ridge crest to scout a Yankee railroad blockhouse. He knew
what he fronted; this was more than a drunken bully—a
really dangerous man.

That queer little moment of silence lengthened, shutting
the two of them up—alone. Drew could not really name the
emotion he felt. Deliberately he tried to subdue the sensation as he turned to the girl.

"What's the matter?"

At first glance he might have thought her a boy, for she
wore hide breeches and boots, a man's shirt now hanging

loosely about her hips. She jerked her head, and a thick braid flopped from under her wide-brimmed hat.

"*Señor, por favor*—please—we have done no wrong. We are the Trinfans—Teodoro and me. Teodoro, he finds *Señor* Juanito's purse in the road, he follows to give it back. He is not a *bandido*—he is not *espía*, a spy one. We are mustangers. Ask of *Don* Reese, of *Señor* Kells. Why, *Señor* Juanito, do you say Teodoro spy on you, why you hit him with the whip?"

"Not thief, not spy!" The boy beside Drew dropped a wealed hand from his face. "The man who says Teodoro Trinfan is *ladrón*—bad one—him I kill!"

Drew's left arm swept out across the boy's chest, pinning him back against the stable.

"Now, what's your story?" the Kentuckian asked the man he fronted.

"An' jus' what's all this smokin' 'bout?" Kells came out. "You, Shannon, what're you doin' here? Been drinkin' again, fightin', too, by th' look of you."

"*Señor* Kells." The girl caught at the older man's arm. "*Por favor, señor,* we are not thieves, not spies. We come after *Señor* Juanito because he dropped his purse. Then he see Teodoro coming, he not listen—he beat on him with quirt. You know, we are honest peoples!"

"Now then, Faquita, don't you git so upset, gal!" She was wailing aloud, making no effort to wipe away the tears running down her cheeks. "Johnny, what kinda game you tryin'? You know these kids are straight; them an' their ol' man's come to work th' Range for wild ones on Rennie's own askin'. Takin' a quirt to th' kid, eh?" Kells' voice slid up the scale. "You sure have yourself a snootful tonight!

Now you jus' walk yourself outta here on th' bounce. I'm doin' th' sayin' of what goes on, on my own property."

"You do a lotta sayin', Kells." The scowl was gone; Shannon's battered mouth was actually smiling. But, Drew decided, he liked the scowl better than the smile and the tone of the voice accompanying it. "Some men oughtta put a hobble on their tongues. Sure, I know these young whelps an' their pa too. Sniffin' round where they ain't wanted. An' mustangers ain't above throwin' a sticky loop when they see a hoss worth it. We ain't blind on th' Range." His head swung a little so he was looking at the girl. "You'd better hold that in mind, gal. Double R hosses have come up missin' lately. It's easy to run a few prime head south to do some moonlight tradin' at th' border. An' we don't take kindly to losin' good stock!"

The boy lunged against Drew's pinioning arm. "Now he says we are horse thieves! Tell that to us before the *Don Cazar!*"

Shannon curled the quirt lash about his wrist. "Don't think I won't, Mex! He don't like havin' his colt crop whittled down. You—" Those blue eyes, brilliant, yet oddly shallow and curtained, met Drew's for the second time. "Don't know who you are, stranger, but you had no call to mix in. I'll be seein' you. Kinda free with a gun, leastwise at showin' it. As quick to back up your play?"

"Try me!" The words came out of Drew before he thought.

Why had he said that? He had never been one to pick a fight or take up a challenge. What was there about Shannon that prodded Drew this way? He'd met the gamecock breed before and had never known the need to bristle at their crowing. Now he was disturbed that Shannon could prick him so.

Odd, the other had been successfully turned from his purpose here. Yet now as he swung around and walked away down the alley Drew was left with a nagging doubt, a feeling that in some way or other Shannon had come off even in this encounter. . . . But how and why?

Teodoro spat. His sister tugged at Kells' sleeve. "It is not true what he said. Why does he wish to make trouble?"

"Lissen, gal, an' you, too, Teodoro—jus' keep clear of Johnny Shannon when he's on th' prod that way. I've knowed that kid since he didn't have muscle enough to pull a gun 'less he took both hands to th' job. But he's not needin' any two hands to unholster now. An' he's drinkin' a lot—mean, ugly drunk, he is. Somethin' must have riled him good tonight—"

"In the cantina there was a soldier from the camp," Faquita volunteered. "They call names. He and *Señor* Juanito fight. *Don* Reese, he put them both out in the street. *Señor* Juanito he falls, drops purse. Teodoro picks it up, and we follow. When we try to give it back *Señor* Juanito yell, 'spy,' hit with whip. That is the truth, *por Dios,* the truth!"

"Yeah, sounds jus' like Johnny these days. Him with a snootful an' somebody yellin' Reb and Yank. Some men can't forgit an' don't seem to want to. Johnny sure takes it hard bein' on th' losin' side—turned him dirt mean. Now, you kids, you stayin' in town?"

"*Sí.*" Faquita nodded vigorously. "With Tía María."

"Then you git there an' stay clear of Johnny Shannon, *sabe?* No more trouble."

"*Sí, Señor* Kells. You, *señor,*" she spoke to Drew, "to you we owe a big debt. Come, Teodoro!" She caught at her brother and pulled him away.

"What makes a kid go sour?" Kells asked of the shadows beyond rather than of Drew. "Johnny warn't no real trouble 'fore he skinned off to ride with Howard. Sure he was always a wild one, but no more'n a lotta kids. An' he'd answer th' lead rein. 'Course we don't know what happened to him in Texas after th' big retreat th' Rebs made outta here. Could be he larned a lot what was no good. Now he sops up whisky when he hits town an' picks fights, like he didn't git his belly full of that in th' war. You can't never tell how a kid's gonna turn out."

"Hey! Mister Kirby, you better git in here!" Callie hailed from the stable. "Th' mare . . . she's . . ."

Drew jammed the Colt under his belt and ran.

The scent of hay, of grain, of horse . . . Drew's head rolled on the pillow improvised from hay and blanket as sun lay hot across his face. He rubbed the back of his hand over his eyes and then came fully awake to remember the night before.

It took only a minute to get down the ladder into Shadow's stall where a broom tail jiggled up and down above absurdly long baby legs and small rounded haunches. Shadow's small daughter breakfasted. Callie squatted on his heels near-by watching the process benignly.

"Ain't she 'bout th' best-favored filly you ever saw?" he asked. "How come all your hosses is grays? Shiloh her pa?"

Drew shook his head. "No, her sire's Storm Cloud. But all that line are grays."

"This Storm Cloud, he's a runnin' hoss?"

"About the runnin'est horse in his part of the country,

Callie. This filly ought to pick up her heels some, if she takes after her dam and sire."

"What you namin' her?"

Up to that moment Drew had not really thought about it. The crisp air blowing into the stable, carrying something beside the scents of the town, gave him a suggestion.

"How about Sage, Callie?"

The boy thought seriously and then nodded. "Yeah— Sage. That's gray an' it's purty, smells good, too."

Drew pulled up his shirt, dug into the pocket of the money belt for the horse papers. "Got a pencil—or better— pen and ink around here anywhere?"

"Mister Kells, he keeps ledgers over in th' tack room. Got some ink an' a pen there. How come you need that? You ain't makin' out no bill of sale on her already, are you?" Callie was shocked.

"Hardly. Just want to put her down right and proper on the tally sheet."

The boy followed to watch Drew make the record on the margin of Shadow's papers. As the Kentuckian explained, Callie was deeply interested.

"You mean as how you can tell way back jus' what hosses bred your hosses? That's sure somethin'! Round here we knows a good hoss, but we ain't always sure of his pa, not if he's wild stuff."

"Lots of wild horses hereabouts then?"

"Sure. Some're jus' mustangs; other's good stuff gone wild—run off by th' 'Paches an' broke loose, or got away from a 'wet hoss' band—"

" 'Wet horse' band?"

Callie glanced at him a little sharply. "How come you

ain't knowin' 'bout 'wet hosses'? Heard tell as how they have 'em that same trouble down Texas way—"

"But I don't come from the border country."

"Well, Texas sure is a great big piece o' country, so maybe you don't know 'bout them river tricks. Wet hosses—they's hosses what is run off up here, driven down to th' border where they's swapped for hosses what some Mex *bandidos* have thrown a sticky loop over. Then th' Mexes take them Anglo hosses south an' sell 'em, where their brands ain't gonna git nobody into noose trouble. An' th' stolen Mex hosses, they's drove up here an' maybe sold to some of th' same fellas what lost th' others. Hosses git themselves lost 'long them back-country trails, specially if they's pushed hard. So them strays join up with th' wild ones. Iffen a mustanger can rope him one an' bring it in . . . well, if it's a good one, maybe so he'll git a reward from th' man what's lost him. Heard tell that *Don* Cazar, he's set some good rewards on a coupla studs as was run off th' Range this summer."

"*Don* Cazar has good horses?"

" 'Bout th' best in these here parts. He runs 'em on th' Range th' old style—stud an' twenty—twenty-five mares together in a *manada,* all one color to a band. They sure is a grand sight: band o' roans, then one o' duns, an' some blacks. He's got one *manada* all of grullas. Sells some to th' army, drives more clear to Californy. An' th' old *Dons* down in Sonora come up once in a while to pick them out some fancy saddle stock. He sure would enjoy seein' these grays o' yours. Iffen you ever want to sell, *Don* Cazar'd give you top price."

"But I'm not sellin'." Drew folded the piece of paper he

had been waving to dry the ink and put it back in the belt pocket. "What's that?"

He could almost believe he heard an army bugle, but the call it sounded was unlike any cavalry signal he had known. Callie was already on his way to the door.

"Wagon train's comin'!" he cried as he ran out.

Drew lingered by Shadow's box. The filly was resting in the straw, her match-stick legs folded under her, and the mare was munching the extra feed of oats the Kentuckian had tipped in for her. He could hear the sound of other running feet outside. It would seem that all Tubacca was turning out to welcome the wagon train of traders from the south. Drew's curiosity got the better of him. He went on out to the plaza.

3 ❅

ONLY A WELL-ARMED and convoyed set of wagons with a highly experienced and competent master could dare travel the Apache-infested trails these days. The first of the freighters, pulled by a sixteen-mule team, fairly burst into the plaza, outriders fanning about it. One of the mounted men was dressed in fringed buckskin, his shoulder-length hair and bushy black beard the badge of a frontier already passing swiftly into history. He rode a big black mule and carried a long-barreled rifle, not in the saddle boot, but resting across the horn as if even here in Tubacca there might be reason for instant action.

The mule trotted on to the middle of the plaza. Then the weapon pointed skyward as its owner fired into the air, voicing a whoop as wild as the Rebel Yell from the throat of a charging Texas trooper.

He was answered by cries and shouts from the gathering crowd as five more wagons, each with a trailer hooked to its main bulk, pulled in around the edge of the open area, until the center of the town was full and the din of braying mules was deafening.

Drew retreated to the roofed entrance of the Four Jacks.

The extra step of height there enabled him to get a good look at two more horsemen pushing past the end wagon. Both wore the dress of Mexican gentlemen, their short jackets glinting with silver braid and embroidery; their bridles, horse gear, and saddles were rich in scrolls and decorations of the same metal. Navajo blankets lay under the saddles, and serapes were folded over the shoulder of one rider, tied behind the cantle of the other.

They pulled up before the cantina, and one man took the reins of both mounts. If the riders' clothing and horse furnishings were colorful, the horses themselves were equally striking. One was a chestnut, a warm, well-groomed red. But the other . . . Drew stared. In all his years about the stables and breeding farms of Kentucky, and throughout his travels since, he had never seen a horse like this. Its coat was pure gold, a perfect match to one of the eagles in his money belt. But the silky locks of mane and tail were night black. Its breeding was plainly Arab, and it walked with a delicate pride as gracefully as a man might foot a dance measure.

Drew had a difficult time breaking his gaze from the horse to the man dismounting. The ranchero was tall, perhaps an inch or so taller than Drew, and his body had the leanness of the men who worked the range country, possessing, too, a lithe youthfulness of carriage. Until one looked directly into his sun-browned face he could pass as a man still in his late twenties.

But he was older, perhaps a decade older than that, Drew thought. Too high and prominent cheekbones with slight hollows below them, and a mouth tight set, made more for strength of will and discipline of feeling than conventional good looks. Yet his was a face not easily forgotten, once seen. Black hair was pepper-salted for a finger-wide space above his ears, which were fronted by long sideburns, and black brows were straight above dark eyes. In spite of his below-the-border dress and his coloring, he was unmistakably Anglo, just as the man looping both horses' reins to the rack was Mexican.

"So, you're still wearing your hair in good order? No trouble this trip?" Topham had come to the door of the cantina, his hand outstretched. "Welcome back, Hunt!"

"Paugh!" The Mexican spat. "Where is there one Indio who is able to face *Don* Cazar on his own ground? The folly of that they learned long ago."

Don Cazar smiled. That mask of aloofness was wiped away as if he were ten years younger and twenty years less responsible than he had been only seconds earlier. "And if they did not beware our rifles, Bartolomé here would talk them to death! Is that not so, *amigo?*" His speech was oddly formal, as if he were using a language other than his own, but there was a warmth to the tone which matched that sudden and surprising smile.

Topham's arm went about the shoulders under the black-and-silver jacket, drawing *Don* Cazar into the light, music, and excitement of the cantina. While Drew watched, the stouter back of Bartolomé cut off his first good look at his father.

So . . . *that* was *Don* Cazar—Hunt Rennie! Drew did not know what he had expected of their first meeting. Now he could not understand why he felt so chilled and lost. He had planned it this way—no demands, no claims on a stranger, freedom to make the decision of when or how he would see his father; that was the only path he could take. But now he turned slowly away from that open door, the light, the laughter and singing, and walked back toward the stable, loneliness cutting into him.

Tubacca had slumbered apathetically before; now the town was wide awake. In a couple of days the wagon train would head on north to Tucson, but now the activity in the plaza was a mixture of market day and fiesta. Small traders from Sonora took advantage of the protection afforded by *Don* Cazar's outriders and had trailed along with their own products, now being spread out and hawked.

Parrots shrieked from homemade cages; brightly woven fabrics were draped to catch the eye. As he wandered about viewing cactus syrup, sweet, brown panocha-candy, fruit, dried meat, blankets, saddles, Drew was again aware of the almost strident color of this country. He fingered appreciatively a horn goblet carved with intricate figures of gods his Anglo eyes did not recognize. The hum of voices, the bray of mules, the baa-ing and naa-ing of sheep and goats, kept up a roar to equal surf on a seacoast. Afternoon was fast fading into evening, but Tubacca, aroused from the post-noon siesta, was in tumult.

A fighting cock tethered to a cart wheel stretched its neck to the utmost in an attempt to peck at Drew's spurs. He laughed, attracted, wrenched out of his own private world. The smell of spicy foods, of fruit, of animals and people . . . the clamor . . . the sights . . .

Drew rounded one end of a wagon and stepped abruptly into yet another world and time. All the stories which had been dinned warningly into his ears since he had left the Mississippi now brought his hand to one of the Colts at his belt. Most of the half-dozen men squatting on their heels about a fire were three-quarters bare, showing dusty, brown bodies. Two had dirty calico shirts loose above hide breechclouts. Dark-brown eyes, as unreadable as Johnny Shannon's, surveyed Drew, but none of the Indians moved or spoke.

Common sense took over, and Drew's hand dropped from the gun butt. Hostiles would not be camping peacefully here in the heart of town. He could not be facing wild Apaches or Navajos. But they were the first Indians he had seen this close since he had ridden out of Texas.

"Somethin' buggin' you, boy?"

Drew's war-trained muscles took over. He was in a half crouch, the Colt flipped over and out, pointing into the shadows where the newcomer emerged. Then the Kentuckian flushed and slammed his weapon back into the holster. This was the buckskinned man who had whooped the train into town that morning.

"Mite quick to show your iron, ain't you?" There was a chill in the question, and Drew saw that the long rifle was still held at alert by its owner.

"Cat-footin' up on a man ought to make you expect somethin' of a reception," Drew countered.

"Yep, guess some men has sure got 'em a bellyful of lead doin' that." To Drew's surprise the other was now grinning. "You huntin' someone?"

"No, just lookin' around." Drew longed to ask some things himself, but hesitated. Frontier etiquette was different from Kentucky custom; it was safer to be quiet when not sure.

"Wal, thar's aplenty to see tonight, right enough. Me—I'm Crow Fenner; I ride scout fur th' train. An' these here—they're Rennie's Pimas, what o' 'em is runnin' th' trail this trip."

So these were the famous Pima Scouts! No wonder they

took their ease in the Tubacca plaza. Every man, woman, and child in those adobe buildings had reason to be thankful for their skill and cunning—the web of protection Rennie's Pima Scouts had woven in this river valley.

"I'm Kirby, Drew Kirby." He hastened to match one introduction with another. "This is my first time in the valley—"

"From th' east, eh?"

"Texas."

"Texas . . ." Something in the way Fenner repeated that made it sound not like a confirmation but a question. Or was Drew overly suspicious? After all, as Callie had agreed last night, the late Republic of Texas was a very large strip of country, housing a multitude of native sons, from the planting families of the Brazos to the ranchers in crude cabins of the Brasado. There were Texans and Texans, differing greatly in speech, manners, and background. And one did not ask intimate questions of a man riding west of the Pecos. Too often he might have come hunting a district where there was a longer distance between sheriffs. What a man volunteered about his past was accepted as the truth.

"Rode a far piece then," Fenner commented. "Me, I've been trailin' round this here country since th' moon was two-bit size. An' I ain't set my moccasins on all o' it yet. Thar's parts maybe even an Injun ain't seed neither. You jus' outta th' army, son?"

Drew nodded. Apparently he could not escape that part of his past, and there was no reason to deny it.

"Iffen you be huntin' a job—*Don* Cazar, he's always ready to hire on wagon guards. Any young feller what knows how to handle a gun, he's welcome—"

"Can't leave Tubacca, at least for now. Have me a mare

over in the livery that just foaled. I'm not movin' until she's ready to travel—"

"Must be right good stock," Fenner observed. "Me, I has me a ridin' mule as kin smell Apaches two miles off. Two, three times that thar mule saved m' skin fur me. Got Old Tar when he turned up in a wild-hoss corral th' mustangers set over in th' Red River country—"

"I saw him when you rode into town. Good-lookin' animal."

Crow Fenner nodded vigorously. "Shore is, shore is. *Don* Cazar, he's partial to good stock—favors Tar, too. Th' *Don* has him a high-steppin' hoss every hoss thief in this here territory'd like to run off. Bright yaller—"

"Saw that one, too. Unusual colorin' all right."

"He put a white stud—white as milk—to run with some light buckskin mares back 'fore th' war. First colt out of that thar breedin' was that Oro hoss. Never got 'nother like him; he's special. Shows his heels good, too. They's gonna race him out on th' flats tomorrow if anyone is fool 'nough to say as he has a hoss as can beat Oro. Thar's always some greenhorn as thinks he has—"

"Oh?" Drew wondered aloud. The black-and-gold horse was beautiful and plainly of good breeding. That he was also a runner was not out of the question. But that Oro could best Gray Eagle-Ariel stock on the track, Drew doubted. There were unbroken records set on eastern tracks by horses in Shiloh's direct blood line. And the local talent that had been matched against Oro in the past had probably not been much competition. The Kentuckian began to speculate about a match between the gray stallion and the horse foaled on the Arizona range.

"Yep, we'll see some race, does anyone turn up with a hoss t' match Oro."

One of the shirted Indians rose to his feet. With rifle sloped over forearm, he padded into the dark. Fenner's relaxed posture tensed into alert readiness. His head turned, his attitude now one of listening concentration. Drew strained to see or hear what lay beyond. But the noise from the plaza and torchlight made a barrier for eye and ear.

Fenner's rifle barrel dropped an inch or so; he stood easy again. Drew heard a jingle of metal, the creak of saddle leather, the pound of shod hoofs.

"Soldiers!" Fenner sniffed. "Wonder what they's doin', hittin' town now. Wal, that ain't no hair off m' skull. Me, I'm gonna git Tar his treat. Promised him some time back he could have a bait o' oats—oats an' salt, an' jus' a smidgen o' corn cake. That thar mule likes t' favor his stomach. Kells, he ought t' have them vittles put together right 'bout now. This mare o' yourn what's so special, young feller . . . Me, I'd like t' see a hoss what's got to be took care of like she was a bang-up lady!"

He put two fingers to his lips and whistled. A mule head, attached to a rangy mule body, weaved forward to follow dog-at-heel fashion behind the scout.

A squad of blue coats was riding in—an officer and six men. They threaded their way to the cantina where the officer dismounted and went inside. The troopers continued to sit their saddles and regard the scene about them wistfully.

"Looks like a duty patrol," Fenner remarked. "Maybe Cap'n Bayliss. He's gittin' some biggety idear as how it's up t' him t' police this here town. Does he start t' crow too loud, *Don* Cazar or Reese Topham'll cut his spurs. Maybe he sets up th' war shield an' does th' shoutin' back thar in front o' all them soldier boys. In this town he ain't no gold-lace general!"

"Troops and the town not friendly?" Drew asked.

"Th' soldiers—they ain't no trouble. Some o' 'em have their heads screwed on straight an' know what they's doin' or tryin' t' do. But a lot o' them officers now—they come out here wi' biggety idears 'bout how t' handle Injuns, thinkin' they knows all thar's t' be knowed 'bout fightin'—an' them never facin' up to a Comanche in war paint, let alone huntin' 'Paches. 'Paches, they know this here country like it was part o' their own bodies—can say 'Howdy-an'-how's-all-th'-folks, bub?' t' every lizard an' snake in th' rocks. Ain't no army gonna pull 'em out an' make 'em fight white-man style.

"*Don* Cazar—he goes huntin' 'em when they've come botherin' him an' does it right. But he knows you think Injun, you live Injun, you eat Injun, you smell Injun when you do. They don't leave no more trail than an ant steppin' high, 'less they want you should foller them into a nice ambush as they has all figgered out. Put Greyfeather an' his Pimas on 'em an' then leg it till your belly's near meetin' your backbone an' you is all one big tired ache. Iffen you kin drink sand an' keep on footin' it over red-hot rocks when you is nigh t' a bag o' bones, then maybe—jus' maybe —you kin jump an Apache. Comanches, now, an' Cheyenne an' Kiowa an' Sioux ride out to storm at you—guns an' arrows all shootin'—wantin' to count coup on a man by hittin' him personal. But th' 'Pache ain't wastin' hisself that way. Nope—git behind a rock an' ambush . . . put th' whole hell-fired country t' work fur them. That's how th' 'Pache does his fightin'. An' th' spit-an'-polish officers what come from eastward—they's got t' larn that. Only sometimes they ain't good at larnin', an' then they gits larned—good an' proper. Hey, Kells!"

They were at the stable and Fenner lifted a hand, palm out, in greeting to the liveryman. "Here's Ole Tar wantin' his special grub—"

Drew went on to Shiloh's stall. Reese Topham, the Spaniard *Don* Lorenzo who had been in the cantina last night, the stout Mexican Bartolomé, and *Don* Cazar himself were all there before him.

"Here he is now." Reese Topham waved a hand at Drew. "This is Mister Kirby, from Texas."

"You have a fine horse there, Kirby—the mare, too. Eastern stock, I would judge, perhaps Kentucky breeding?" Rennie asked.

Drew was taut inside. To say the wrong thing, to admit the line of that breeding, might be a bad slip. Yet he could only evade, not lie directly.

"Yes, Kentucky." He answered the first words his father had ever addressed to him.

"And the line?"

To be too evasive would invite suspicion. However, the Gray Eagle get was in more than one Kentucky stable.

"Eclipse . . ." Drew set back the pedigree several equine generations. Shiloh tossed his head, looked over his shoulder at Drew, who entered the stall and began quieting the stallion with hands drawn gently over the back and up the arch of the neck.

"The mare also?" *Don* Cazar continued.

"Yes." The Kentuckian's answer sounded curt in his own ears, but he could not help it.

"This Eclipse, *amigo*," *Don* Lorenzo turned to Rennie for enlightenment—"he was a notable horse?"

"*Sí,* of the Messenger line. But a gray of that breeding—" *Don* Cazar's forefinger ran nail point along his lower lip. "Ariel blood, perhaps?"

Drew busied himself adjusting Shiloh's hackamore. This was getting close. Hunt Rennie had lived in Kentucky over a year once. He had visited Red Springs many times before he had dared to court Alexander Mattock's daughter and been forbidden the place. His visits to the stable must have familiarized him with the Gray Eagle-Ariel strain bred there. On the other hand, horses of the same combination were the pride of several other families living around Lexington.

"A racing line of high blood," *Don* Lorenzo said thoughtfully. "*Sí,* this one has the pride, the appearance. You have raced him, *señor?*" he asked Drew with formal courtesy.

"Not on any real track, *señor*. During the war there were no races."

"He wasn't a cavalry mount?" *Don* Cazar looked surprised.

"No, suh. Too young for that. He was foaled on April sixth in sixty-two. That's why they called him Shiloh."

There was a moment of silence, broken by a hail from the door.

"You there—Rennie!"

Drew saw the involuntary spasm of *Don* Cazar's lips, the shadow of an expression which might mean he anticipated a distasteful scene to come. But the quirk disappeared as he turned to face the man in the blue uniform.

"Captain Bayliss." It was acknowledgment rather than a greeting, delivered in a cool tone.

"I want to see you, Rennie!" The officer stamped forward a step or so, to stand in the full light of the first lantern. He was of medium height, and his blue blouse had been cut by a good tailor, though now it was worn. He was a good-looking man, though jowly about the mouth, above which a closely cropped mustache bristled. His color was high under a pink skin which in this hot country must burn painfully. And there was the permanent stamp of uncertain temper in the lines about his prominent eyes.

4 ✻

"So, you see me, bayliss," *Don* Cazar returned evenly. "There is some trouble?"

Bartolomé shifted from one foot to the other, his spurs ringing. *Don* Lorenzo's expression was one of withdrawal, but on the round countenance of the Mexican was open dislike.

The sun-reddened skin flushed darker. "All right, Rennie!" the captain exploded. "If you want it straight, that's the way you're going to get it! You've been hiring Rebs again!"

Once before Drew had seen explosive anger curbed visibly by a man who knew the folly of losing control over his emotions. It had been on a hilltop back in Tennessee, with the storm clouds of January overhead. General Bedford Forrest, watching men driven to the limit by necessity and his own orders, had looked just that way when he had rounded on Drew, bearing news of yet another breakthrough by the Federals. Now it was this Anglo wearing Spanish dress and standing in a dim stable, reining temper to meet the open hostility of the captain.

"Captain Bayliss." The words sounded as remote as if the

44

speaker bestrode some peak of the Chiricahuas to address a pygmy in a canyon below. "I know of no law which states that I may not employ whom I choose on my own land. If a man does his job and makes no trouble, his past does not matter. I am as ready to fire a former Union soldier as I am a Confederate—"

"I tell you again: I'm not going to have Rebs around here passing on information to Kitchell!"

"And *I* say once again, Captain, that men who ride for me do not in addition ride for Kitchell."

"*Sí*—!" Bartolomé's face was as flushed as Bayliss' now. "We do not help those *bandidos*. Do they not also raid us? Two weeks ago Francisco Perez, his horse comes in with blood on the saddle. We ride out and find him—shot, dragged with the rope. That is not Apache trick, that, but the work of Kitchell and his snakes!"

"Peace, *amigo*." *Don* Cazar's raised finger silenced his man. "Bartolomé is right, Bayliss. Kitchell is beginning to nibble at the Range. He has not many sources of supply left. Soon he will either have to cross the border to stay or make some reckless raid which will give us a chance at him."

"These damned Rebs around here will keep him going! You can't tell me they don't back him every chance they get. And I'm warning you, Rennie, if you hire any man you can't answer for, he's going to the stockade and you'll hear about it from the army!"

"And you also listen, Captain. I will not be dictated to, and the army had best understand that. I do not want Kitchell in this country any more than you do. He has made a boast of being Confederate leading what he terms Mounted Irregulars. But to my knowledge he never held a commission from the South, and he is nothing but an out-law trading on the unsettled state of the territory. That is recognized by every decent man in Arizona. And that covers those you call 'Rebels' as well as former Union men."

Bayliss was silent for a long second, and then he jerked his hat farther down on his peeling forehead. "You've had notice, Rennie, that's all I have to say. I'm going to clear all the Rebs out of this section. Then we will be able to get at Kitchell, and the army will settle him for good and all!"

"Bayliss!" The captain had half turned, but *Don* Cazar's call halted him. "Don't you try harassing any of my riders. They mind their business and will not make any trouble as long as they are left in peace. If there are any problems in town, *Don* Lorenzo Sierra, here, is the alcalde and they must be referred to him."

The captain favored Rennie with a last glare and was gone. Tobe Kells spoke first.

"That one's chewin' th' bit an' gittin' ready to hump un-der th' saddle. This business of tryin' to run out th' Rebs, it'll cause smokin'!"

"He has no right to give such an order," *Don* Cazar was beginning when the alcalde interrupted:

"*Compadre,* for a man such as that your talk of rights means nothing. He is eaten by the need to impress his will here, and that will bring trouble. I do not like what I have heard, no, I do not like it at all."

"You know what may be really eating at him this time, Hunt?" Topham spoke from where he was leaning against the wall of Shadow's box stall. "Johnny was throwing his weight around again last night. Had a set-to in the Jacks with a trooper. Unless the kid quits trying to fight the war over again every time he sees an army blouse—or until he

stops pouring whisky down him every time he hits town—
there may be shooting trouble. There're some equal hot-
heads in Bayliss' camp, and if Johnny goes up against one
of them, a scuffle could become a battle."

"Yeah, an' that warn't all Johnny was doin' last night."
Kells shifted his tobacco cud from one cheek to the other.
"Iffen Kirby here hadn't been to hand, Johnny would have
skinned th' Trinfan kid with his quirt—jus' 'cause he
dropped his purse outside th' Jacks an' th' kid followed him
to give it back. Johnny's meaner than a drunk Injun these
days. That's Bible-swear truth, Rennie."

"To lose a war makes a man bitter," *Don* Cazar said
slowly. "Johnny was far too young when he ran away to
join Howard. And after that defeat at Glorieta, the retreat
to Texas was pure hell with the fires roaring. It seems to
have done something to the boy—inside."

"Johnny wasn't the only boy at Glorieta. From what I've
heard most of them weren't old enough to grow a good
whisker crop." Topham's voice had lost its detached note.
"And he sure wasn't the only Confederate to surrender.
Hunt, he's got to learn that losing a war doesn't mean that
a man has lost the rest of his life. But the way he's been
acting these past months, Johnny might just lose it. Bayliss'
tongue is hanging out a yard or more he's panting so hard
to get back at you. That captain has heady ambitions under
his hat, maybe like setting up here as a tinpot governor or
something like. If he can discredit you, well, he probably
thinks he's got a chance to rake in the full pot, and it's a
big one. Get Johnny back on the Range, Hunt—put him to
work, hard. Sweat that sour temper and whisky out of
him. He used to be a promising youngster; now he's turning bronco fast. All he seems to have learned in the war

is how to use those guns of his to lord it over anyone he believes he can push around. And someday he'll try to push the wrong man—"

Don Cazar was staring ahead of him now at Drew and Shiloh. But Drew knew that Hunt Rennie was not seeing either man or horse, but a mental picture which was not too pleasing.

"He's just a boy." Rennie did not utter that as an excuse; rather he said it as if to reassure himself. Then his eyes really focused on Drew, and he changed the subject abruptly.

"Kirby, when the train comes in we sometimes set up a race or two. Any thought of trying your colt against some of the local champions?"

"Oro perhaps?" Drew counter-questioned.

Rennie laughed. "Oh, so you've been talking, Fenner?"

The scout came away from where Tar was still very audibly munching his treat. "Didn't know as how th' younker had him a runnin' hoss, *Don* Cazar." He inspected Shiloh critically. "But that thar sure looks a lotta hoss. 'Course maybe he ain't used t' runnin' out here whar th' ground ain't made all nice an' easy fur his feet. But I dunno, I dunno at all."

"Anyway he'll give Oro stiffer competition than he's had in the last two races. Unless that Lieutenant Spath up at the camp tries again with that long-legged black of his," Topham added. "What about it, Kirby? You willing to match Shiloh?"

"He's green, but, yes, I'll do it."

Drew's motives were mixed. His pride in the colt had been pushing him toward such a trial ever since he had heard Fenner speak of Oro. In addition, as the owner of a noted horse, he would take a place in this community, establish his identity as Drew Kirby. And in some way he could not define, this put him, at least in his own mind, on an equal footing with *Don* Cazar.

But by the next morning a few doubts troubled him as he tightened saddle cinches on the stallion. Shiloh's only races so far had been impromptu matches along the trail. Though the colt had been consistently the victor, none of his rivals had been in his class. And if Oro's speed was as striking as his coloring, the Range stud would prove a formidable opponent.

"Walk him up and down here by the corral." The Kentuckian handed the reins to Callie. "Got something I have to do."

Drew went directly to the Four Jacks. This time the cantina was filled, with a double row of the thirsty demanding attention at the bar. But Topham was seated at a table with *Don* Lorenzo and Zack Cahill of the stage line. The Kentuckian went over to them.

"You have come to back your horse, *señor?*" *Don* Lorenzo smiled up at Drew. There were piles of coins on the table as Cahill listed bets for the men crowding around.

"Yes, suh." Drew spun down two double eagles. "What're the odds?"

"Started six to one for Oro," Topham told him. "Coasted down after a few of the boys had a look at Shiloh. Can give you four to one now. Anything else we can do for you?"

Drew dropped his voice. "Do you have a safe here?"

Topham's eyebrows climbed. "Do you foresee a deposit or a withdrawal?"

"Deposit. I want to ride light today."

"Then I'll admit possession of a safe, such as it is. *Don*

Lorenzo, *por favor,* will you act as banker?" He beckoned
Drew after him into a small back room which was in sharp
contrast to the main part of the Four Jacks.

On one wall was a fanned display of old daggers and
swords which dated a century or so back to the Spanish
colonial days. A bookcase crammed with tightly squeezed
volumes provided a resting place for pieces of native pot-
tery bearing grotesque animal designs. On the far wall were
strips of brightly colored woven materials flanking a huge
closed cupboard, a very old one, Drew thought. Its paneled
front was carved with deeply incised patterns centering
about a shield bearing arms. Only the battered desk and an
attendant chair with a laced rawhide seat were of the
frontier.

Topham took a chained key from the pocket of his fancy
vest and went to fit it into a lock concealed in the carved
foliage of the cupboard. The shield split down the middle, revealing shelves of metal boxes and packets of papers.
Drew unfastened his money belt and handed it over. As he
was tucking his shirt in his belt once more the gambler
nodded at the cupboard.

"This is about as near a bank as we boast in Tubacca.
Cahill has a strongbox at the stage station, and Stein some
kind of a lockup at his store—that's the total for the town.
We haven't grown to the size for a real banking establishment—"

"Hey, Reese, th' Old Man about—?"

Shannon was in the doorway. In the full light of day he
looked younger. Drew was puzzled. That strange animosity
which had flashed between them last night—why had he
felt it? There was nothing like that emotion now. But as
Johnny Shannon's gaze flitted from Topham to the Ken-

tuckian, Drew was once more aware that, whatever he might outwardly seem, Johnny Shannon was no boy. Behind that disarmingly youthful façade was another person altogether.

"Kirby, ain't it?" Shannon smiled. "Understand I got outta line th' other night . . . stepped on a lotta toes." That gaze flickered for the merest instant to the Colts at the Kentuckian's belt. "I sure had me a real snootful an' I guess I was jus' fightin' th' war all over again. No hard feelin's?"

That guileless confession was very convicing on the surface. How did you assess an emotion you did not understand yourself? Drew was teased by a fleeting memory of the past, of a time when he had faced another pair of eyes such as those, surface eyes behind which you could see nothing. Then he became conscious that the pause was too lengthy, and he replied with a hurry he immediately regretted:

"No hard feelin's."

This time he was able to recognize the meaning of that quirk of Shannon's lips. But prudence controlled the small flare of temper he felt inside him. It did not really matter. Let Shannon think he was backing down. If the time ever came that they did have to have a showdown, Johnny Shannon might be the surprised one.

"You're sure a trustin' fella." Shannon's fingers hooked to the front of the gun belt riding low on the hip. "Not askin' for no receipt or nothin' . . ."

Topham laughed. "We don't forget what is due a customer, Johnny." He went to the desk, scribbled a line on a piece of paper, and held it out to Drew. "This should meet all contingencies, such as some patron out there getting downright ornery and putting a couple of extra buttonholes in my vest by the six-gun slug method."

"Heard tell as how you're fixin' to race your plug 'gainst Oro, Kirby," Johnny drawled. "Also as how you laid down some good round boys to back his chance. I took me a piece of them—easy pickin's." The sneer was plainer in his voice than it had been in his smile.

Drew's puzzlement grew. Why was Shannon leaning on him this way? Because he had stepped in to stop the quirting of Teodoro? That was the only reason the Kentuckian could think of.

"That's a matter of opinion." Topham was studying them both with interest. "I'd say Oro has him some real competition at last. None of the Eclipse blood was ever backward on the track."

"You ridin' yourself?" Shannon paid no attention to the gambler's comment.

Drew nodded. "He knows me, and I ride light—"

"Sure, I suppose you do—now." Shannon's eyes flickered again, this time to the locked cupboard. "Heard tell—least-ways Callie's been spoutin' it around—that you was with General Forrest."

"Yes."

"You sure musta pulled outta th' war better'n th' rest of us poor Rebs. Got you a couple of blooded hosses an' a good heavy money belt. A sight more luck than th' rest of us had—"

"Don't include yourself in the empty-pocket brigade, Johnny," Topham rapped out. "I don't see you going without eating money, drinking money either, more's a pity. And if you're really looking for Rennie now, you'll find him down at the course."

Shannon's smile was gone. He straightened away from the door frame which had been supporting his shoulders. "Thanks a lot, Reese." He left with the same abruptness as he had from the stable alley.

"So you're riding yourself." Topham ignored the departure. "León Rivas, Bartolomé's son, will be up on Oro; he always rides for Rennie. He's younger than you, but I'd say"—the gambler studied Drew's lithe body critically—"you're about matched in weight. I'd shuck that gun belt, though, and anything else you can. And good luck, Kirby. You'll need all of it you can muster."

An hour later Drew followed Topham's advice, leaving gun belt, carbine, and everything else he could unload in Callie's keeping before he swung up on Shiloh. The big colt was nervous, tending to dance sideways, tossing his head high. Drew concentrated on the business at hand, striving to forget the crowd opening up to let him through, shouting encouragement or disparagement. Ahead was the appointed track, a beaten stretch of earth, part of the old road leading to the mines. The Kentuckian talked to Shiloh as they went, keeping up a stream of words to firm the bond between horse and rider.

There was a knot of men surrounding the golden horse, and as his rider mounted, Oro put on a good show, rearing to paw the air with his forefeet as if he wished nothing better than to meet his gray rival in an impromptu boxing match. Then he nodded his head vigorously, acknowledging the shouts from his enthusiastic supporters. Beside that magnificent blaze of color Shiloh was drab, a shadow about to be put to flight by the sun.

They were to break at a starting shot, head to the big tree which made an excellent landmark in the flat valley, rounding its patch of shade before returning to the starting point. Drew brought Shiloh, still prancing and playing with his bit, up beside Oro. The slim boy on the golden horse shot the Kentuckian a shoulder-side look and grinned, raising his quirt in salute as Drew nodded and smiled back.

Some of the noise died. *Don* Lorenzo pointed a pistol skyward. Drew strove to make his body one with Shiloh's small easy movements. The big gray knew very well what was in progress, was tensing now for a swift getaway leap. And he made it on the crack of the gun.

But if Shiloh had easily outdistanced all opposition before on those improvised tracks, he was now meeting a far more equal race. The gray colt's stride was effortless, he was pounding out with power—more than Drew had ever known him to exert. Yet those golden legs matched his pace, reach for reach, hoofbeat for hoofbeat.

"Come on, boy!" Drew's urging was lost in the wild shouting of the spectators. Some who were mounted were trying to parallel the runners. But Shiloh responded to his rider's encouragement even if he could not hear or understand. Drew would never use quirt or spur on the stud. What Shiloh had to give must come willingly and because he delighted in the giving.

They swept in and around the shade of the tree, made the arc to return. That golden head with its tossing crown of black forelock; it *was* slipping back! Oro was no longer nose to nose with Shiloh, rather now nose to neck. Drew could hear Rivas' voice encouraging, pleading . . .

A mass of men, mounted and on foot, funneled the runners down to where the line of rope lay straight to mark the finish. Oro was creeping up once more, inch by hard-won inch.

Drew's head went up, his throat was rasped raw by the Yell which had taken desperate gray-coated troopers down hedge-bordered roads in Kentucky and steep ravines in Tennessee, sending them, if need be, straight into the mouths of Yankee field guns. And the Yell brought Shiloh home, only a nose ahead of his rival—as if he had been spurred by the now outlawed war cry. Then Drew found he had his hands full trying to pull up the colt and persuade him that the race was indeed over.

5 ✳

A BLACK MULE came up beside Drew as he slowly pulled Shiloh down to a canter. Fenner, a wide grin splitting his beard, bellowed:

"That shore was a race! Need any help, son?"

Drew shook his head, wanting to bring Shiloh under full control at a rate which would quiet the colt before they headed back to the furor about the finish line. And only now did he have time to relish his own excited pride and pleasure.

Since he had first seen Shiloh on that scouting trip back to Kentucky in '64, he had known he must someday own the gray colt. He had lain out in the brush for a long time that morning to watch the head groom of Red Springs put the horse through his paces in the training paddock. And watching jealously, Drew had realized that Shiloh was one of those mounts that a man discovers only once in his lifetime, though he may breed and love their kind all his years.

Drew would have been content with Shiloh as a mount and a companion, but now he was sure that the colt was more, so much more. This gray was going to be one of the Great Ones, a racer and a sire—to leave his mark in horse history and stamp his own quality on foals throughout miles and years in this southwestern land. Drew licked the grit of dust from his lips, filled his lungs with a deep breath as Shiloh turned under rein pressure.

It was a long time before the Kentuckian was able to separate Shiloh from his ring of new admirers and bring him back to the stable. Drew refused several offers for the colt, some of them so fantastic he could only believe their makers sun-touched or completely carried away by the excitement of the race.

But when he found *Don* Cazar waiting for him at Kells', he guessed that this was serious.

"You do not wish to sell him, I suppose?" Hunt Rennie smiled at Drew's prompt shake of head. "No, that would be too much to hope for, you are not a fool. But I have something else to suggest. Reese Topham tells me you are looking for work, preferably with horses. Well, I have a contract to gentle some remounts for the army, and I need some experienced men to help break them—"

Drew could not understand the sudden pinch of—could it be alarm? Here it was: a chance to work on the Range, to know Hunt Rennie, and learn whether *Don* Cazar was to remain a legend or become a father. But now he was not sure.

"I'm no breaker, suh. I've gentled, yes—but eastern style."

"Breaking horses can be brutal, though we don't ride with red spurs on the Range. Suppose we try some of the eastern methods and see how they work on our wild ones. Do you think you can do it?"

"A man can't tell what he can do until he tries." Drew still hedged.

There was a trace of frown now between Rennie's brows.

"You told Topham you wanted work." His tone implied that he found Drew's present hesitancy odd. And—from *Don* Cazar's point of view—it was. Tubacca was still in a slump; the rest of the valley held about as many jobs for a man as Drew had fingers on one hand. The Range was the big holding, and to ride there meant security and an established position in the community. Also, perhaps it was not an offer lightly made to an unknown newcomer.

"I can't promise you blue-grass training, suh. That has to begin with a foal." He hoped Rennie would credit his wavering to a modest appraisal of his own qualifications.

"Blue-grass training?"

As his father repeated the expression Drew realized the slip of tongue he had made. And if he took the job, there might be other slips, perhaps far more serious ones. But to refuse, after Topham had spoken for him . . . he was caught in a pinch with cause for suspicion closing in on either side.

"I was in Kentucky for about a year after the war. I went to stay with a friend—"

"But you *are* from Texas?"

Was Rennie watching him too intently? No, he must ride a tighter rein on his imagination. There was no reason in the wide world why *Don* Cazar should expect him to be anyone except Drew Kirby.

"Yes, suh. Didn't have anythin' to go back to there. Thought I'd try for a new start out here." There was the story of several thousand veterans. Rennie should have heard it a good many times already.

"Well, come and try some blue-grass training on our colts. And should you let this stud of yours run with a picked *manada* of mares, I could promise good fees."

"Suppose I said yes if the fees were some of the foals—of my own choosing, suh?" Drew asked.

Rennie ran a finger across the brand which scarred the gray's hide. "Spur R—that's a new one to me."

"My own. Heard tell as how there's a custom of the country that a slick this old can be branded and claimed by anyone bringing him in. I wasn't going to lose him that way should he do any straying, accidental or intentional."

Don Cazar laughed. "That's using your head, Kirby. All right. It's a deal as far as I'm concerned. You draw wrangler's pay and take stud fees in foals—say one in three, your choosing. Register that brand of yours with *Don* Lorenzo to be on the safe side. Then you're welcome to run Spur R with the Double R on the Range."

He held out his hand, and Drew grasped it for a quick shake to seal their agreement. He was committed now—to the Range and to a small partnership with its master. But he still wondered if he had made the right choice.

Two days later he dropped bedroll and saddlebags on the spare bunk at one end of the long adobe-walled room and studied his surroundings with deep curiosity. It was a fort, all right, this whole stronghold of Rennie's—not just the bunkhouse which formed part of a side wall. Bunkhouse, feed store, and storage room, blacksmith shop, cookhouse, stables, main house, the quarters for the married men and their families—all arranged to enclose a patio into which choice stock could be herded at the time of an attack, with a curbed well in the center.

The roofs of all the buildings were flat, with loopholed parapets to be manned at need. A sentry post on the main house was occupied twenty-four hours a day by relays of Pimas. A loaded rifle leaned at every window opening, ready to be fired through loopholes in the wooden war shutters. The walls were twenty-five inches thick, and mounted on the roof of the stable, facing the hills from which Apache attacks usually came, was a small brass cannon—*Don* Cazar's legacy from troops marching away in '61.

What he saw of the resources of this private fort led Drew to accept the other stories he had heard of the Range, like the one that *Don* Cazar's men practiced firing blindfolded at noise targets to be prepared for night raids. The place was self-contained and almost self-supporting, with stores of food, good water, its own forge and leather shop, its own craftsmen and experts. No wonder the Apaches had given up trying to break this Anglo outpost and Rennie had accomplished what others found impossible. He had held his land secure against the worst and most unbeatable enemy this country had nourished.

There were other Range forts, smaller, but as stoutly and ingeniously designed, each built beside a water source on Rennie land—defense points for *Don* Cazar's riders, their garrisons rotated at monthly intervals. And Drew had to thank that system for having taken Johnny Shannon away from the Stronghold before the Kentuckian arrived. Rennie's foster son was now riding inspection between one water-hole fortification and another. But Drew was uncertain just how he would rub along with Shannon in the future.

"*Señor* Kirby, *Don* Cazar—he would speak with you in the Casa Grande," León Rivas called through one of the patio side windows.

"Coming." Drew left the huddle of his possessions on the bunk.

The Casa Grande of the Stronghold was a high-ceilinged,

five-room building about sixty feet long, the kitchen making a right angle to the other rooms and joining the smoke house to form part of another wall for the patio. Mesquite logs, adze-hewn and only partially smoothed, were placed over the doorways, and the plank doors themselves were slung on hand-wrought iron hinges or on leather straps, from oak turning-posts. Drew knocked on the age-darkened surface of the big door.

"Kirby? Come in."

Here in contrast to the brilliant sunlight of the patio was a dusky coolness. There were no glass panes in the windows. Manta, the unbleached muslin which served to cover such openings in the frontier ranches, was tacked taut, allowing in air but only subdued light. The walls had been smoothly plastered, and as in Topham's office, lengths of colorful woven materials and a couple of Navajo blankets served as hangings. Rugs of cougar and wolf skin were scattered on the beaten earth of the floor. There was a tall carved cupboard with a grilled door, a bookcase, and two massive chests shoved back against the walls. And over the stone mantel of the fireplace hung a picture of a morose-looking, bearded man wearing a steel breastplate, the canvas dim and dark with age and smoke.

Don Cazar was seated at a table as massive as the chests, a pile of papers before him flanked by two four-branch candelabra of native silver. Bartolomé Rivas' more substantial bulk weighed down the rawhide seat of another chair more to one side.

"Sit down—" Rennie nodded to the seat in front of the table. "Smoke?" He pushed forward a silver box holding the long cigarillos of the border country. Drew shook his head.

"Whisky? Wine?" He gestured to a tray with waiting glasses.

"Sherry." Drew automatically answered without thought.

"What do you think of the stock you saw down in the corral?" *Don* Cazar poured a honey-colored liquid from the decanter into a small glass.

As the Kentuckian raised it to sip, the scent of the wine quirked time for him, making this for a fleeting moment the dining room at Red Springs during a customary after-dinner gathering of the men of the household. The talk there, too, had been of horses—always horses. Then Drew came back in a twitch of eyelid to the here and now, to Hunt Rennie watching him with a measuring he did not relish, to Bartolomé's round face with its close-to-hostile expression. Deliberately Drew sipped again before answering the question.

"I'd say, suh, if they're but a sample of Range stock, the breed is excellent. However——"

"However what, *señor?*" Bartolomé's eyes challenged Drew. "In this territory, even in Sonora, there are none to compare with the horses of this hacienda."

"That is not what I was about to say, *Señor* Rivas. But if *Don* Cazar wishes to try the eastern methods of training, these horses are too old. You begin with a yearling colt, not three-year-olds."

"To break a foal! What madness!" Now Bartolomé's face expressed shock.

"Not breaking," Drew corrected, "training. It is another method altogether. One puts a weanling on a rope halter, accustoms him to the feel of the hackamore, of being with men. Then he grows older knowing no fear or strangeness."

The Mexican looked from Drew to *Don* Cazar, his shock fading to puzzlement. Rennie nodded.

"*Sí, amigo,* so it is done—in Kentucky and Virginia. But this time we must deal with the older ones. Can you modify those methods, gentle without breaking? A colt with the fire still in him, but saddle-broke, is worth much more—"

"I can try. But you have already said, suh, that you don't allow rough breakin' here." Drew's half suspicion crystallized into belief. *Don* Cazar had not really wanted another wrangler at all; he had wanted Shiloh—and his foals. Well, perhaps he would find he did have a wrangler who could deliver the goods into the bargain.

"No, but it is always well to learn new ways. I have been in Kentucky, Kirby. Perhaps some of their methods would not work on the Range. On the other hand, others might. As you have said—we can but try." He picked up the top sheet of paper and began to read:

"*Bayos-blancos*—light duns—two. *Bayos-azafranados*—saffrons—one. *Bayos-narajados*—orange duns—none——"

"There was one," Bartolomé interrupted. "The mare, she was lost at Cañon del Palomas."

Rennie frowned, "*Sí,* the mare. *Bayos-tigres*—striped ones —three. *Bayos-cebrunos*—smoked duns—two. *Grullas*— blues—four. Roans—six. Blacks—three. Bays—four. Twenty-five three-year-olds. You won't be expected to take on the whole *remuda,* Kirby. Select any six of your own choosing and use your methods of gentling on them. We'll make a test this way."

Bartolomé uttered a sound closer to a snort than anything else. And Drew guessed how he stood with the Mexican foreman. Rennie might have faith, or pretend to have faith, in some new method of training, but Rivas was a conservative who preferred the tried and true and undoubtedly considered the Kentuckian an interloper.

"Now, the matter of Shiloh . . ."

Drew finished the sherry with appreciation. He was beginning to see the amusing side of this conference. Drew's work on the Range settled, Rennie was about to get to what he really wanted. But *Don* Cazar's first words were a little startling.

"We'll keep him close—in the water corral. To turn a stud of eastern breeding loose is dangerous——"

"You mean he might be stolen, suh?" Drew clicked his empty glass down on the table.

"No, he might be killed!" And Rennie's tone indicated he meant just that.

"How . . . why?"

"There are wild-horse bands out there, though we're trying to capture or run them off the Range. And a wild stud will always try to add mares to his band. Because he has fought many times to keep or take mares, he is a formidable and vicious opponent, one that an imported, tamed stud can rarely best. Right now, coming into Big Rock well for water is a pinto that has killed three other stallions—including a black I imported back in '60—and two of them were larger, heavier animals than he.

"The Trinfans are moving down into that section this week. I hope they can break up that band, run down the stud anyway. He has courage and cunning, but his blood is not a line we want for foals on this range. So Shiloh stays here at the Stronghold; don't risk him loose."

"Yes, suh. What about these wild ones—they worth huntin'?"

"They're mixed; some are scrubs, inbred, poor stuff. But

a few fine ones turn up. Mostly when they do they're strays or bred from strays—escaped from horse thieves or Indians. If the mustangers here pick up any branded ones, they're returned to the owners, if possible, or sold at a yearly auction. By the old Mexican law the hunting season for horses runs from October to March. Foals are old enough then to be branded. Speaking of foals, you left your mare and the filly in town?"

"Kells'll give them stable room till next month. I can bring them out then."

"We'll have a delivery of remounts to make to the camp about then. You can help haze those in and pick up your own stock on return."

León appeared in the doorway. *"Don* Cazar, the *mesteneoes*—they arrive."

"Good. These people are the real wild-horse experts, Kirby. Not much the Trinfans don't know about horses." *Don* Cazar was already on his way to the door and Drew fell in behind Bartolomé.

The Trinfan outfit was small, considering the job they intended, Drew thought. A cart pulled by two mules, lightly made and packed high, was the nucleus of their small caravan. Burros—two of them—were roped behind and, to Drew's surprise, a cow, bawling fretfully and intended, he later learned, to play foster mother to any unweaned foals which might be picked up. The cart was driven by a Mexican in leather breeches and jacket over a red shirt. Behind him rode the boy and girl Drew had seen in the Tubacca alley, mounted on rangy, nervous horses that had speed in every line of their under-fleshed bodies. Each rider trailed four spare mounts roped nose to tail.

"Buenos días, Don Cazar." For so small a man the Mex-

ican on the cart seat produced a trumpet-sized voice. He
touched the roll-edged brim of his sombrero, and Drew
noted that his arm was crooked as if in the past it had been
broken and poorly set.

"*Buenos días, Señor* Trinfan. This house is yours." Rennie went to the side of the cart. "The west corral is ready
for your use as always. Draw on the stores for any need
you may have—"

"*Gracias, Don* Cazar." It was the thanks of equal to equal.
"You have some late news of the wild ones?"

"Only that the pinto still runs near the well."

"That spotted one—*sí,* he is an Apache for cunning, for
deviltry of spirit. It may be that this time he will not be
the lucky one. There is in him a demon. Did I not see him,
with my own eyes, kill a foal, tear flesh from the flanks of
its dam when she tried to drop out of the run? *Sí*—a real
diablo, that one!"

"Get rid of him one way or another, Trinfan. He is a
danger to the Range. He killed another stud this season.
I am as sure of that as if I had seen him in action."

"Ah, the blue one you thought might be a runner to
match Oro. *Sí,* that was a great pity, *Don* Cazar. Well, we
shall try, we shall try this time to put that *diablo* under!"

An hour later Drew was facing a *diablo* of his own, with
far less confidence than Hilario Trinfan had voiced. Just
how stupid could one be? Around him now were men
trained from early childhood to this life, and he could show
no skill at their employment. All the way out from Texas
he had practiced doggedly with the lariat, and his best fell
far short of what a range-bred child could do.

Yet he had an audience waiting down at the corral.
Drew's mouth was a straight line. He would soon confirm

their belief that *Don* Cazar had in truth hired Shiloh instead of his owner. But there was no use trying to duck the ordeal, and the Kentuckian had never been one to put off the inevitable with a pallid hope that something would turn up to save him.

Only this time, apparently, fortune was going to favor him.

"Which one you wish, *señor?*" Teodoro Trinfan, rope in hand, stood there ready to cast for one of the milling colts. Why the boy was making that offer of assistance Drew had no inkling. But to accept would give him a slight chance to prove he could do part of the work.

He had already made his selection in the corral, though he had despaired of ever getting that animal at rope's end.

"The black—"

6 ✳

He worked in the dust of the smaller corral, with Croaker's help, adapting his knowledge of eastern gentling the way he had mentally planned it during the days since he had accepted the job. With the excited and frightened colt roped to the steady mule Drew tried to think horse, feel horse, even be horse, shutting out all the rest of the world just as he had on the day of the race. He must sense the colt's terror of the rope, his horror of the strange human smell—the man odor which was so frightening that a blanket hung up at a water hole could keep wild horses away from the liquid they craved.

Drew talked as he had to Shiloh, as if this black could understand every word. He twitched the lead rope, and Croaker paced sedately about in a wide circle, dragging the colt with him. Drew then reached across the bony back of the mule, pressed his hand up and down the sweaty, shivering hide of the black. No hurry, must not rush the steady, mild gesture to the horse that here was a friend.

The Kentuckian had no idea of the passing of time; it was all part of the knowledge that slow movements, not swift ones, would prevent new panic. The blanket was shown, allowing the black to sniff down its surface, before it was flapped back and forth across the colt's back, and finally left there. Now the saddle. And with that cinched into place, the black stood quietly beside Croaker.

Drew mounted the mule and rode. The saddled black, loosened from the twin tie, followed the mule twice around the corral. The rider dismounted from Croaker, was up on the black. For perilous seconds he felt flesh and muscles tense under his weight; then the body relaxed.

His hand went up. "Open the gate!" he called softly.

Seeming to realize he was free of the pole walls, the black exploded in a burst of speed which was close to Shiloh's racing spurt. Drew let him go. Three-quarters of an hour later he rode back, the black blowing foam, but answering the rein.

He found *Don* Cazar, Bartolomé, and Hilario Trinfan waiting for him by the corral. The mustanger walked forward with a lurch, his head thrown far back so he could look up at Drew from under the wide brim of his sombrero.

"This you could not do with a true wild one," he commented.

"I know that, *señor*. This colt was not an enemy, one who has already been hunted by man. He was only afraid. . . ."

"But you have the gift. It is born in one—the gift. A man has it, and the horse always knows, answers to it. Ride with me, *señor,* and try that gift on the wild ones!"

"Someday—" That was true. Someday Drew did want to ride after the wild ones. Anse's stories of horse hunting on the Texas plains had first stirred that desire. Now it was fully awake in him.

Don Cazar inspected the black closely. "Well, Bartolomé, what have you to say now?"

"*Señor* Kirby knows his business," the Mexican admitted. "Though I think also that this was no true wild one. He will make a good remount, but he is no fighter such as others I have seen here."

Drew unsaddled and left the black in with Croaker; he fed both animals a bait of oats. In the morning he would be at this again. And he still had not solved the problem of roping. He could not expect Teodoro to come to his aid a second time. He started slowly back to the bunkhouse.

"*Señor*—?"

Drew raised his wet head from the bunkhouse basin and reached out for a sacking towel. "Yes?"

León sat on a near-by bunk. "I have thought of something—"

"Sounds as if it might be important," Drew commented.

"*Don* Cazar, he has offered money—a hundred dollars in gold—to have off the Range that killer pinto stud. But that one, he is like the Apache; he is not to be caught."

"Can't someone pick him off with a rifle?"

"Perhaps. Only that has also been tried several times, *señor*. My father, he thought he had killed him only two months ago. But the very next week did not the pinto come to steal mares from the bay *manada*? It must have been that he was only creased. No, he is a *diablo*, and he hides in the rocks where he cannot easily be seen. But there is a plan I have thought of—" León hesitated, and Drew guessed he was about to make a suggestion which he believed might meet with disapproval.

"And this plan of yours?" Why had León come to him

with it? Surely young Rivas had better and closer friends at the Stronghold. Why approach a newcomer?

"That pinto—he is a fighter; he likes to fight. He will not allow another stud on the ground he claims."

Drew was beginning to understand. Wild ones were sometimes trapped by a belled mare staked out to draw them in. But a stud to catch a fighting stud was another plan altogether.

"You would offer him a fight?"

"*Sí*, but not a real fight. Just allow him to believe that there would be one. Pull him so out of hiding in the rocks—"

"Using what stud for bait?"

"*Señor* Juanito—he said a stud that would fight too, like Shiloh."

"Shiloh!" Drew wadded the towel in his fist and pitched it across the room. "Shiloh!"

León must have read something of Drew's blazing anger in his face, for the Mexican's mouth went a little slack and his hand came up in an involuntary gesture as if to ward off a blow.

"It is a good plan!" His boy's voice was thin in protest against Drew's expression.

"It is a harebrained, dangerous scheme," began Drew; then he switched to a question. "Did Johnny Shannon suggest using Shiloh for bait, or was that your idea?"

"*Señor* Juanito—he said one must have a good horse, a fighter. But such a horse would not be hurt. We would wait with rifles and shoot the pinto quickly before he attacked. There would be no harm to Shiloh, none at all. *Señor* Juanito said that. Only a trick to get the *diablo* where we could shoot. Maybe—" León's eyes dropped, a flush rose slowly on his brown cheeks—"maybe it was very foolish. But when *Señor* Juanito told it, it sounded well."

"Did he tell you to ask me about it?"

The flush darkened. "He did not say so, *señor*. But one would not do such a thing without permission. Also, you should be one of the hunters, no? How else could we go?"

"Well, there won't be any huntin' of that kind, León. Trinfan knows what he's doin', and I don't think that pinto is goin' to be runnin' loose—or alive—much longer."

Drew pulled a clean shirt over his head. What kind of game was Johnny Shannon trying to play? Apparently he had almost talked León into using Shiloh as bait in this fool stunt. Had he expected the kid to take the horse without Drew's knowledge? Or for some reason had he wanted León to spill this? A trick to get Shiloh out of the Stronghold? But why?

He buckled on his gun belt, settled the twin holsters comfortably. Shannon—what and why, he repeated silently. Nothing sorted out in his mind. Drew only felt a prickle of uneasiness which began between his shoulder blades and ran a chill down his spine, as if rifle sights were on him.

But Shannon did not return to the Stronghold, and Drew was kept busy at the corrals from dawn to dusk. In a month of hard work it was easy to forget what might only be fancies.

There was an invigorating crispness in the air, and the dun gelding the Kentuckian rode savored the breeze as a desert dweller savors water. Drew was indulgent with his mount's skittishness as they pounded along at the tail of the horse herd bound for Tubacca.

From a rocky point well before them there was a flash of

light. Jared Nye, on Drew's left, took off his hat and waved a wide-armed signal to answer Greyfeather's mirror. Two of the Pimas were scouting ahead on this two-day drive, and the Anglo riders were keeping the herd to a trot. Apaches, Kitchell, even *bandidos* from over the border, could be sniffing about the Range, eyeing its riches, ready to pick up anything left unprotected. The men rode with their rifles free of the boot, fastened by a loop of rawhide to the saddle horn, the old Texas precaution which allowed for instant action. And at each halt the six-shooter Colts' loading was checked.

Nye swerved, sending a lagger on with a sharp crack of quirt in the air. He pulled up to match Drew's sobered trot.

"That's the last bad stretch; now it'll be downhill an' green fields all th' way." Nye nodded at the narrow opening between two hills lying ahead. "Glad to get this band in on all four legs an' runnin' easy."

"You expected trouble?"

"Kid, in this here country you don't expect nothin' else but. Last time we brought hosses up th' trail they jumped us four, five miles back—right close to where we saw that pile of bones this mornin'. 'Fore he knew what hit us Jim Berry was face down an' never got up again. An' th' Old Man took him a crease 'crost th' ribs that made him bleed like a stuck pig. Got him patched up an' into town; then he keeled over when he tried to git down off his hoss an' was in bed a week."

"Apaches?"

"Naw, we figured it was Kitchell. Couldn't prove it though, an' after that th' Old Man made a rule we take Pimas every drive. Ain't nothin' able to surprise them. I never had no use for Injuns, but these here are peaceful cusses—iffen they don't smell an Apache. With them ridin' point we're sure slidin' th' groove. Me, I'll be glad to hit town. I'd shore like to keep th' barkeep busier than a beaver buildin' hisself a new dam. Though with th' Old Man off reppin' for th' law down along the border and needin' hands back on the Range, we swallows down th' dust nice an' easy an' takes it slow. Anyway, this far from payday I kin count up mosta m' roll without takin' it outta m' pocket."

"This Kitchell . . . think it's true that some of the ranchers are really helpin' him?"

"Don't know. Might be he's tryin' to play th' deuce against th' whole deck. Lessen he lives on th' kind of whisky as would make a rabbit up an' spit in a grizzly's eye hole, he's got somethin'—or someone—to back him. Me . . . were th' Old Man poundin' th' hills flat lookin' for me, I'd crawl th' nearest bronc an' make myself as scarce as a snake's two ears." Nye shrugged. "Kitchell's got some powerful reason for squattin' out in th' brush playin' cat-eyed with most of th' territory. Maybe so there're some as will sit in on his side, but they've sure got their jaws in a sling an' ain't bawlin' about it none. 'Course lotsa people were red-hot Rebs back in '61 till they saw as how white men fightin' each other jus' naturally gave th' Apaches an' some of th' border riffraff idears 'bout takin' over. But mosta us now ain't wavin' no flag. Iffen Kitchell has got him some diehards backin' him—" Nye shrugged again. "Git 'long there, you knock-kneed, goat-headed wagon-loafer!" He pushed on to haze another slacker.

They were dusty and dry when they dropped the corral gate in place and watched the horses mill around. Drew headed for Kells' stable. Shadow nickered a greeting and turned around as if to purposefully edge her daughter forward for his inspection.

"Pretty, ma'am," he told her. "Very pretty. She's goin' to be as fine a lady as her ma—I'm willin' to swear to that."

The filly lipped Drew's fingers experimentally and then snorted and did a frisky little dance with her tiny hoofs rustling in the straw. Kells had been as good as his promise, Drew noted. Mother and child had had expert attention, and Shadow's coat had been groomed to a glossy silk; her black mane and tail were rippling satin ribbons.

"Gonna take 'em back to th' Range with you, Mister Kirby?" Callie came down from the loft.

"Yes. I'll need a cart and driver though. We'll have to give the foal a lift. Know anyone for hire, Callie?"

"I'll ask around. Have any trouble comin' up?"

"No. Greyfeather and Runnin' Fox were scoutin' for us."

"Stage was jumped yesterday on th' Sonora road," Callie volunteered. "One men got him a bullet in th' shoulder, but they got away clean. It was Kitchell, th' driver thought. Captain Bayliss took out a patrol right away. You plannin' on goin' back with Kitchell out?"

"Don't know," Drew replied absently. Better leave that decision to Nye; he knew the country and the situation. "You ask about the cart, Callie, but don't make it definite. Have to see how things turn out."

Drew started for the Four Jacks to meet Nye. Back here in Tubacca he was conscious how much he had allowed his personal affairs to drift from day to day. Of course he had seen very little of Hunt Rennie at the Stronghold; his father had ridden south on patrol with his own private posse shortly after his own arrival there. But whenever Drew thought seriously of the future he had that odd sense of dislocation and loss which he had first known on the night he had seen *Don* Cazar arrive at the cantina. *Don* Cazar— Hunt Rennie. Drew Kirby—Drew Rennie. A seesaw to make a man dizzy, or maybe the vertigo he felt was the product of too much sun, dust, and riding.

There was someone at a far table in the cantina, but otherwise the dusky room was empty. Drew went directly to the bar. "Got any coffee, Fowler?"

"Sure thing. Nye was in here 'bout five minutes ago. Said for you to wait here for him. You hear 'bout Kitchell holdin' up th' stage?"

"Callie told me. Said the army patrol went out after him."

"Yeah, don't mean they'll nail him though. He's as good as an Apache 'bout keepin' undercover. Here's your coffee. Want some grub, too?"

The smell of coffee revived Drew's hunger. "Sure could use some. Haven't eaten since we broke camp at sunup."

"Sing's in th' kitchen. I'll give him th' sign to rattle th' pans. Say—been racin' that Shiloh of yours lately? Sure am glad I played a hunch an' backed him against Oro." Fowler's red forelock bobbed over his high forehead as he nodded vigorously.

"No racin' on the Range."

"Hope you're keepin' him closer. That border crew'd sure like to git a rope on him! Down Sonora way one of them Mexes would dig right down to th' bottom of his money chest to buy a hoss like that. I'll go an' tell Sing."

Drew, coffee mug in hand, sat down at a table where some of the breeze beat in the door now and then. Lord, he was really tired. He stretched out his legs, and the sun made twinkly points of light on the rowels of the Mexican spurs. Sipping the coffee, he allowed himself the luxury of not doing any thinking at all.

Fowler brought a heaping plate and Drew began to eat.

"Oh, there you are!" Nye slammed in, swung one of the chairs about, and sat on it back to front, his arms folded across the back.

"You ridin' out to tell the army we're here—with the horses?" Drew asked.

"Nope, caught sight of them ridin' in. Looked like Sergeant Muller was in command—he'll come in here. Hey, Fowler, how's about another plate of fodder?"

"Steady on, fella. Make it straight ahead now!"

Both of them looked up. A burly man wearing sergeant's stripes steered a slighter figure before him through the open door. Johnny Shannon, a bandage about his uncovered head, lurched as if trying to free himself from the other's grip and caught at a chair back. Nye and Drew jumped up to ease him into a seat.

"What's—?" began Nye.

Muller interrupted. "Found him crawlin' along right near town. Says as how he was took by Kitchell 'n' got away, but he ain't too clear 'bout what happened or where. Wearin' a crease 'longside his skull; maybe that scrambled up his thinkin' some."

"Better get Doc Matthews. I think he's in town." Fowler came from the bar, a glass in hand.

"Right. I'll go." Nye started out.

Johnny had slumped forward, his head on the table encircled by his limp arms. Drew was puzzled. Shannon was supposed to have ridden south on the Range, not north. What was he doing this far away from the water-hole route? Had he found a trail which led him in this direction? Or had he been jumped somewhere by Kitchell's pack of wolves and forced along for some purpose of their own?

"Was he ridin', Sergeant?" Drew asked, hardly knowing why.

"No—footin' it. Said somethin' about Long Canyon after we gave him a pull at a canteen. Sure came a long way if that's where he started."

"I'll go get Hamilcar. He knows somethin' 'bout doctorin'," Fowler cut in. "Maybe Doc Matthews ain't here, after all."

"Hey, Sarge, can I see you a minute?" came a hail from without.

"You manage." Muller made it more order than request as he left.

Drew sat alone with Shannon, one hand on the boy's shoulder to steady him. He was aware of movement behind him. If the fellow at the back table had been dozing earlier, he was roused now.

"Where did you git them spurs?"

Drew turned, his lips shaped a name, tried again, and got it out as a hoarse whisper. "Anse! Don't you know me, Anse?"

He saw eyes lift from the floor level, the scarred cheek under a ragged fringe of beard; and then astonishment in the other's expression became a flashing grin.

"Drew—Drew Rennie! Lordy, it's sure enough Drew Rennie!"

Drew was on his feet. His hands on the other's shoulders pulled him forward into a rough half embrace. "Anse!" He swayed to the joyous pounding of a fist between his shoulder blades. "I thought you were dead!" he somehow gasped.

"An' I seen *you* go down; a slug got you plumb center!"

the Texan sputtered. "Rolled 'round a bush an' saw you git it! But for a ghost you're sure lively!"

"Caught me in the belt buckle," Drew recounted that miracle of the war. "Knocked me out; didn't really touch to matter, though."

Anse pushed away a little, still holding Drew tightly by the upper arms. "Anybody told me I'd see Drew Rennie live an' kickin', I'd said straight to his face he was a fork-tongued liar!"

Drew came partly to his senses and the present. Fowler . . . Nye . . . either one of them could come back on this reunion. "Anse—listen! This is important. I ain't Drew Rennie—not here, not now—"

"Had to draw a new name outta th' deck?" Anse's grin faded; his eyes narrowed. "All right, what's the goin' handle?"

"Kirby, Drew Kirby . . . I'll explain later." He had given the warning only just in time. Fowler and Hamilcar were coming from the back room of the cantina, and there was a stir at the table.

Johnny was sitting up, his head swaying from side to side, his eyes on Drew and Anse. But the stare was unfocused; he must still be only half conscious. Drew had a fleeting prick of worry. Had Shannon heard anything he would remember? There was nothing to be done about that now.

7 ✳

". . . AND THAT'S THE WAY IT IS." Drew sat on the stool which was the only other furnishing in the bath cubicle while Anse splashed and wallowed in the slab tub.

The Texan swiped soap from his cheek. "An' ain't you gonna tell?"

"I don't know. Would you?"

"Go with m' hat in hand an' say, 'Well, Pa, here's your wanderin' boy'? No, I dunno as how I'd be makin' that kinda play neither. Never was one to unspool th' bedroll till I was sure o' th' brand I was ridin' for. An' you an' me's kinda hide-matched there. Glad you wised me up in time."

"Maybe I didn't," Drew admitted.

"You mean that Shannon? I know you think he's filin' his teeth for you, but I'd say he was too busy countin' stars from that skull beltin' to make sense out of our hurrawin'. I'll give him th' eye though. Lissen now, you're Kirby— so am I called for a rebrandin', too? Seems like two Kirbys turnin' up in a town this size is gonna make a few people ask some questions."

"You're my cousin—Anson Kirby." Drew had already thought that out. "Now, you've some tall talkin' to do your ownself. I saw you roll out of your saddle back in Tennessee. How come you turn up here and now?"

Anse sluiced water over his head and shoulders with cupped hands.

"Do I tell it jus' like it happened, you'll think I'm callin' up mountains outta prairie-dog hills, it's that crazy. But it's range truth. Yeah, I landed outta that saddle on some mighty hard ground. If you'll remember, I had me a hole in the shoulder big enough to let th' wind whistle through. I rolled between th' bushes jus' in time to see you get it —plumb center an' final, so I thought. Then . . . well, I don't remember too good for a while. Next time I was able to take a real interest I was lyin' on a bed with about a mountain of quilts on top me, weaker'n a yearlin' what's jus' been dragged outta a bog hole. Seems like them Yankees gathered me up with th' rest of them bushwacker scrubs, but when they got me a mile or so down th' road they decided as how I'd had it good an' there was no use wastin' wagon room on me. So they let me lie. . . .

"Only," the Texan paused and then continued more soberly, "Drew, sometimes—sometimes it seems like a hombre can have a mite more'n his share of luck; or else he's got him Someone as is line ridin' for him. We had us friends in Tennessee, an' it jus' happened as how I was dropped where one of them families found me. They sure was good folks; patched me up an' saw me through like I was their close kin. Hid me out by sayin' as how I had th' cholera.

"An' most of th' time I didn't know a rope from a saddle —outta my head complete. First there was that shoulder hole; then I got me a good case of lung fever. It was two months 'fore I could crawl round better'n a sick calf what lost its ma too early. Then, jus' as I got so I could stamp m' boots on th' ground an' expect to stand straight up in 'em, this here Yankee patrol came 'long an' dogged me right into a bunch o' our boys they had rounded up. I had me some weeks in a prison stockade, which ain't, I'm tellin' you, no way for to spend any livin' time. Then this here war was over, an' I was loose. No hoss, no nothin'. Some of th' boys got to talkin' 'bout trailin' back to Texas, tryin' out some ranchin' in the bush country. A lotta wild stuff down there—nobody's been runnin' brands on anythin' much since '61. We planned to get a herd of mavericks, drive up into Kansas or Missouri, an' sell. A couple of th' boys had run stuff in that way for th' army, even swum 'em across the Mississippi. It would maybe give us a start. An'— well, there weren't nothin' else to do. So we tried it." Anse sat staring down at the water lapping at his lean middle. His was a very thin body, the ribs standing out beneath the skin almost as harshly as did the weal of the scar on his shoulder.

"And it didn't work?"

"Well, it might've. I ain't sayin' it won't for some hombres. Only we run into trouble. Texas ain't Texas no more; it's th' Fifth Military District. Any man what fought for th' Confederacy ain't got any rights. It's worse'n an Injun war. We got us our herd, leastwise th' beginnin' of one. An' that was back-breakin' work—we was feelin' as beat as when we run out of Tennessee after Franklin. Only we kept to it, 'cause it would give us a stake. So we started drivin' north, an' they jumped us."

"Who?"

"Yankees—th' brand what probably set at home an' let others do th' real fightin'—ready to come in an' take over once th' shootin' was done with. They grabbed th' herd. Shot Will Bachus when he stood up to 'em, an' made it all legal 'cause they had a tin-horn deputy ridin' with 'em. Well, we got him anyway an' two or three of th' others. But then they called in th' army, an' we had to ride for it. Scattered so they had more'n one trail to follow. But they posted us as 'wanted' back there. So I come whippin' a mighty tired hoss outta Texas, an' I ain't plannin' on goin' back to any Fifth Military District!"

"Any chance they'll push a star after you here?"

"No. I'm jus' small stuff, not worth botherin' 'bout by their reckonin', now I ain't got anythin' left them buzzards can pick offen m' bones. They's sittin' tight an' gittin' fat right there."

"Then it's all set." Drew tossed Anse a towel. "Climb out and we'll get started!"

"Doin' what?"

"You've worked horses, and they can use another wrangler on the Range. Right now they've a lot to be topped—want to gentle 'em some and trade 'em south into Mexico. If you ride for *Don* Cazar, nobody's goin' to ask too many questions."

"How d'you know he'll sign me on?" Anse studied his own unkempt if now clean reflection in the shaving mirror on the wall. "I sure don't look like no bargain."

"You will when we're through with you," Drew began. The Texan swung around.

"Looky here, you thinkin' of grub stakin'? I ain't gonna—"

"Suppose you had yourself a stack of cart wheels and my pockets were to let?" Drew retorted. "I think I remember me some times when we had one blanket and a hunk of hardtack between us, and there weren't any 'yours' or 'mine' about it! Or don't you think back that far?"

Anse laughed. "All right, *compadre,* pretty me up like a

new stake rope on a thirty-dollar pony. If I don't agree, likely you'll trip up m' foreleg an' reshoe me anyway. Right now—I'll say it out good'n clear—I'm so pore m' backbone rattles when I cough."

"Mistuh Kirby—" Hamilcar came in. "Mistuh Nye says to tell you he'll be back. Mistuh Shannon's in bed at th' doctuh's; he's gonna be all right soon's he gets ovah a mighty big headache."

He had actually forgotten Shannon! Hastily Drew expressed his satisfaction at the news and added:

"This is my cousin from Texas, Hamilcar. He hit town ridin' light. I'm goin' over to pick him up a new outfit at Stein's. You give him all the rest, will you?"

"Yes, suh."

Blue blouses—a corporal's guard of troopers—were pulling up by the cantina hitch rail as Drew came out into the plaza. Muller's men probably, he thought. But now he was more intent on Anse's needs.

Few people had ever broken through the crust of self-sufficiency the Kentuckian had begun to grow in early childhood. His grandfather's bitter hatred of his father had made Drew an outsider at Red Springs from birth and had finally driven him away to join General Morgan in '62. Those he had ever cared about he could list on the fingers of one sunbrowned, rein-hardened hand: Cousin Meredith; her son Shelly—who had died at Chickamauga between one short breath and the next—Shelly's younger brother Boyd, who had run away to join Morgan, too, in the sunset of the raider's career; and Anse, whom he had believed dead until this past hour.

Drew was breathing as fast as if he had charged across the sun-baked plaza at a run, when he came into the general store which supplied Tubacca with nine-tenths of the materials necessary for frontier living. He made his selection with care.

"You planning a trip, Mister Kirby?" Stein peered at him over a pair of old-fashioned, steel-bowed spectacles which perched on his sharp parrot's beak of a nose.

"No. My cousin just rode in; he lost his gear on the road and needs a new outfit complete."

Stein nodded, patted smooth the top shirt on a growing pile. "Anything else?"

"Add those up. I'll look around." Drew paused to glance into the single small, glass-fronted case which was Stein's claim to fame in the surrounding territory. The exotic wares on display were a strange mixture: a few pieces of jewelry, heavy Spanish things which might be a century or more old, several six-guns—one with an ornate ivory handle. . . . Drew stopped and pulled a finger across the dusty surface of the glass case. Spurs—silver spurs—not quite so elaborate as those he now wore, but of the same general workmanship.

"I'd like to look at those spurs."

Stein unlocked the case and took them out. As Drew unstrapped those he wore and fitted the new pair to his boots, a brown, calf-bound book thudded to the floor. Books—here in Stein's?

Weighing the volume in his hand, the Kentuckian straightened up. There were two more books lying on the top of the case. The leather bindings were scuffed and one was scored clear across the back, yet they had been handsome, undoubtedly treasured. Drew turned them up to read the scrolled gold titles on their spines.

"*History of the Conquest of Mexico, The Three Mus-*

keteers, The Count of Monte Cristo . . . Where'd these come from, Mister Stein?" Drew's curiosity was aroused.

"That is a story almost as fanciful as the ones inside them." Stein rested his bony elbows on the counter as he talked. "Would you believe, Mister Kirby, these were brought to me by Amos Lutterfield?"

"Lutterfield? Who's he?"

"I forget, you have not been in Tubacca long. Amos Lutterfield—he is what one might term a character, a strange one. He goes out into the wilds alone, seeking always the gold."

"In Apache country?" Drew demanded.

"The Apaches, they do not touch a man they believe insane, and Amos has many peculiarities: peculiarities of dress, of speech, of action. He roams undisturbed, sometimes coming in with relics from the old cliff houses to trade for supplies. Last month he told me a story of a cave where he found a trunk. Where it had come from or why it was hidden he did not know, but these books were in it. Like some men who have no formal education, Amos is highly respectful of the printed word. He thought the books of great value and so brought them here."

Drew opened the top volume. Back home books as well bound as these would have carried a personal bookplate or at least the written name of the owner, but the fly leaf was bare. They had the look of well-read, cherished volumes but no mark of possession.

"You have perhaps read these?" Stein asked.

Drew picked up *The Three Musketeers*. "Not likely to forget this one," he said, grinning. "Earned me a good ten with the cane when I read it instead of dealing faithfully with Caesar's campaigns in Gaul. I did get to finish it before

I was caught out." The pages separated stiffly under his exploring fingers as if the volume had not been opened for a long time. He did not notice that Stein was eyeing him with new appraisal.

"These for sale?"

"In Stein's everything is for sale." The storekeeper named a price, and Drew bargained. When he left, the three books reposed on the top of his armload of clothing, and a half hour later he dropped them down on a cantina table. Anse came from the bathhouse and sat down in the opposite chair. His booted foot moved, but now rowel points flashed in the sun. The Texan regarded the Mexican spurs joyfully, stooped to jingle them with his finger tip.

"Can't believe it . . . how they came back to you," he marveled. "One of them Yankees musta took 'em off me, thinkin' I was cashin' in m' chips. Sure feels good to git 'em back on my heels agin, sorta like they was m' luck. Pa, he set a right lot by them spurs. Gave 'em to me when I gentle broke a wild one none o' th' other boys could back. Was I turkey-cock proud th' first day I rode into town with 'em playin' pretty tunes, even though I strapped 'em on over boots as was only three pieces of leather hangin' to each other restless like. Yeah, Pa, he got 'em in the Mexican War, an' me, I wore 'em mostly through this past ruckus. They's sure seen a lotta history bein' made by men climbin' up an' down from saddles!"

"Let's hope . . . no more wars." Drew set the three books in a pile and regarded them attentively. Stein's story of their origin—out of a trunk hidden in a desert cave—was most intriguing. What else had been in that trunk?

"Anse," he asked, "why would anyone hide a trunk in a cave?"

"Might depend on what was in it," the Texan replied promptly.

"Well, these were—"

Anse took up the top book. His finger traced each word as he read. *"The Three Mus—Musketeers.* Whatever kinda critter is that?"

"A soldier. They used to have them over in France a long time ago."

"Army manual, eh? Maybe so the trunk was an army cache—"

Drew shook his head. "No, this is just a story. A good one with lots of prime fightin' in it. This one's a story, too. I've heard about it . . . never got a chance to read it though." He set *The Count of Monte Cristo* upright on the table. Anse took the third volume.

". . . *Con—Conquest of Mexico.* Hey, conquest means winnin' th' country, don't it? This about the Mex War which our pa's fought?" He flicked open the pages eagerly.

"No, the earlier one—when the Spanish came in under Cortés and broke up the Aztec empire . . . back in the 1500's."

"Kinda stiff readin' . . . looks interestin' though." Anse gave his verdict. "We had us two books. Pa learned us to read outta them. One was th' Bible Ma brought 'long when she was married. T'other—that sure was kinda queer how we got that. Pa was in th' Rangers, an' he had this run-in with some Comanches—" Anse's eyes were suddenly bleak, and Drew remembered the few stark sentences the Texan had once spoken to explain his reason for being in the army—a return to a frontier ranch to find nothing left, nothing he wanted to remember, after the Comanches had swept across the countryside.

"Well," Anse broke that short pause, "Pa shot him one big buck as was ridin' straight into th' Ranger line, wantin' to count one o' them coups by whangin' some white man personal with his lance, or some such foolishness. This buck had him a war shield an' Pa picked it up when all th' smoke blew away. What'd' you think that there shield was packed with? Well, this one had a book all tore apart an' stuffed in between th' front an' back layers of hide. Th' boys in th' company, they got right interested in sortin' out all them pages an' puttin' 'em in order agin, kinda like a game, Pa said. Pa, he never had much schoolin', but he could read good an' write an' figger. He sure liked to read, so he claimed that there book when it was all tied up together agin—'cause he shot th' buck as was carryin' th' shield. So he made a buckskin case and kept all th' pages together. That was 'bout soldiers of th' old time, too—parts of it. Romans they was called. Wonder now—did it maybe go back into a shield agin afterward?" He gazed beyond Drew's shoulder into the world outside the cantina door.

"Why would anyone want to store books in a trunk in a cave?" Drew changed the subject quickly to break that unseeing stare. He outlined what Stein had told him, and Anse's attention was all his again.

"Might catch up with this Lutterfield an' ask a few questions—"

"Stein couldn't get anythin' out of him. Guess the old man is a little addled. Maybe someone was storin' stuff, hopin' to come back when the war was over. Anyway, there's no way to identify the owner or owners—"

Anse picked up *The Three Musketeers*. "You say this is good—'bout fightin' an' such?"

Drew nodded. "Try it . . ."

"Somethin' like this is good t' have. A hombre gits tired readin' labels on cans. I'd like to see how much Pa pushed into m' thick head. Good coverin' this book has. Wouldn't you say as th' hombre that had it was kinda heavy in th' pocket?"

"Yes. In fact, these were bound to order."

"How can you tell that?"

"These two might have come bound alike." Drew pointed to the book Anse held and *The Count of Monte Cristo*. "They were written by the same author and could have been part of a matched set. But this one is on a totally different subject and by another writer—Prescott. Yet it is uniformly bound to match the others. I'd say they came from the personal library of a man able to indulge himself in pretty expensive tastes."

"Makes you think," Anse agreed. "Wonder what else was in that trunk."

"Looky what we've got us here! Regular li'l schoolhouse right in this cantina!"

The table moved an inch or so as a thick body brought up with a rush against it. A hand, matted with sun-bleached hair, made a grab for the book Drew had just laid down. Before the startled Kentuckian could pull it back from that grasp, hand and book were gone, and the trooper who had taken it was reeling back to the bar, waving the trophy over his head.

"Schoolhouse . . . right here . . ." he mouthed. "Sittin' there . . . two li'l boys, studyin' their lessons. Now, ain't that somethin'?"

A chair went over with a crash. Anse was on his feet, had taken two steps in the direction of the soldier. Drew jumped after him, trying to assess the situation even as his hand closed restrainingly on the Texan's shoulder.

There were four troopers. Wide grins on the faces of the three still against the bar suggested they were ready to back their companion in any form of horseplay he intended to try.

"Sam, one o' them thar schoolboys is breathin' down yore neck kinda hot like," the tallest of the bar row observed.

Anse jerked against Drew's hold. There was no expression on his thin face, but the old saber scar from lip to eye on his left cheek was suddenly twice as noticeable.

Sam reached up against the bar, squirmed around, the book still in his hand.

"Wal, now, sonny, you ain't really wantin' this here book back? Never knowed any li'l boy what warn't glad to see th' last o' a book. Better git away from a real man 'fore you gits yore backside warmed. That's what th' teacher does to smarty kids, ain't it?"

"You'd better watch out, Sam." Again the tall man cut in. Sam was still grinning, but there was a curve of lip which was far from any real humor, even that provoked by the practical jokes of a barracks bully. "One of them kids had been sayin' as how he rode with Forrest, regular li'l red-hot Reb, he is. Stomp all over us . . . that's what you Rebs has been promisin' to do, ain't it? Gonna stomp all over any Blue Bellies as comes into this town? Well, we ain't bein' booted—not easy—an' not by you, Reb!"

A second, perhaps more—that much warning Drew had before the speaker lurched from the bar straight for him. What had happened, how this had sprung up out of nothing, the Kentuckian could not understand. But he knew well that he was under an attack delivered with a purpose, and with all the dirty tricks of a no-rules, back-alley fighter.

8 ✳

ONLY ONCE BEFORE, when some river toughs had ganged up on the scouts, had Drew had to use fists to beat his way out of an argument. But that had been a round dance at Court House Day compared to this. Within moments the Kentuckian knew that he was no match for the trooper, that he would be lucky if he could get out of this unmaimed. The fellow knew every dirty trick and was eager to use them all. Drew tried only to keep on his feet and out of the other's grip. Once down, he knew he would have no chance at all.

Then he was jerked back, off balance, staggering on to bring up against the wall. He caught at the solid backing and somehow remained upright, seeing hazily through one eye. The other was puffing closed, and his lip was torn, a trickle of blood rising there to drip down his chin. He put both hands to his middle where more than one of the pile-driver knocks had landed, and tried to understand what was happening.

Sergeant Muller . . . that was Muller standing over the man on the floor. And Nye . . . Reese Topham . . . suddenly the cantina was very well populated. Drew turned his head cautiously to see on his blind side. Anse was down! The Kentuckian stood away from the wall, lurched out to fall to his knees. He rolled the Texan over on his back. Anse's eyes fluttered open, and he looked up dazedly. There was an angry red mark on his chin just an inch or so away from the point of his jaw.

"Now, just what devil's business is goin' on here?" The sergeant's voice was a roar to hurt the ears. Somehow Drew got an arm under Anse's shoulders and tried to hoist him up. The Kentuckian swallowed blood from his lip and glared at Muller.

"Suppose you ask those high-binders of yours!" he snapped. And once more it was Sergeant Rennie who spoke.

Other hands joined his to boost Anse. With Topham's aid Drew regained his feet and got the staggering Texan, still half unconscious, onto a chair.

"I'm interested, too." The cantina owner's drawl was as slow as ever, but it held a note of a whiplash.

"Them soldiers . . ." Fowler appeared, the bar-side shotgun across his arm—"they jumped th' boys. I saw it, myself."

"Yeah, told yuh these town buzzards're all th' same. Stick together an' have it in for th' army!"

Drew could not see which of the troopers had burst out with that, but in his present mood all bluecoats were the enemy.

"Dirty Yanks!" Anse's eyes were fully focused now—right on the sergeant. Anse struggled to get up, but Topham's hands on his shoulders held him down. His hand went to his holster, and Drew's fist came down on the Texan's wrist, hard.

"See that thar, Sarge! Th' stinkin' polecat of a Reb was gonna draw on you! Told you, they's all alike. Th' war ain't

over; we jus' gotta keep on lickin' 'em. Give us room, an'
we'll do it again—now!"

Anse's face was green-white under the weathering, save
for the wound on his jaw. He was watching Muller as if
the sergeant, rather than his men, was the focal point of any
future attack.

"You—Stevens—shut your trap!" Muller's roar brought
silence. Drew could actually hear the panting breaths of
the men now.

"Mitchell, what happened here?" Muller turned to the
man at his far right.

The trooper was younger than the rest, his face still holding something of a boyish roundness. His eyes shifted under
the sergeant's steady, boring stare, and he glanced at the
rest of his companions, the two disheveled fighters, the lanky
man picking up a forage cap and handing it to one of them.

"I dunno, Sergeant. Th' boys . . . they was jus' funnin'.
They didn't meant nothin', jus' funnin'. Then these here
Rebs, they come right after Helms, was gonna jump him
from behind. An' Danny waded in jus' to keep that one"—
the boy pointed straight at Drew—"offa Helms. That's what
happened. Th' boys didn't mean no harm—jus' havin' a little
fun—when these Rebs jumped 'em!"

Drew pulled up his neckerchief and dabbed at his cut
lip. Anse had subsided, though he was still watching the
sergeant with an unrelenting gaze. The Kentuckian tried
to remember where Fowler had been during the fracas. He
had spoken up for them already, but would Muller accept
his testimony over that of his own men? There was already
ill feeling between the army and the town. Drew remembered *Don* Cazar's encounter with Bayliss at Kells' stable.
What had Reese Topham said then? That the captain was

only waiting to make trouble for Rennie. And now here he was himself—one of Rennie's riders—involved in a saloon fight with troopers. Drew began to realize that this could be even worse than the physical punishment he and Anse had suffered.

"You . . . bartender—" The sergeant now looked to Fowler. "What'd you see?"

"You ain't gonna take his word for it, for anythin' in this mudhole of a town, are you, Sarge? They'd all lie their heads off to git a trooper into trouble. Wouldn't you now?" The lanky man sidled along the bar to snarl at Fowler.

"Stevens, shut that big mouth of yours, an' I ain't gonna say that agin! All right, Fowler, tell me what *you* saw!"

Fowler slid the shotgun out of sight, apparently sure that an armistice, at least, was assured.

"Th' boys"—he nodded at Drew and Anse—"were sittin' at that table, mindin' their own business. Helms, he went over an' picked up a book——"

"A book!" Muller's craggy features mirrored astonishment. "What book? Why?"

Topham moved and suddenly they were all watching him. He stooped, picked up the dark-brown volume, and a torn page fluttered to the floor. He gathered that up, too, and tucked it back in the proper place.

"It would seem, Sergeant," he remarked, "that there *was* a book involved. And if your men didn't bring it in here, then Kirby or his friend must have. This is certainly not a cantina fixture. Hmm, *History of the Conquest of Mexico*," he read the title on the cracked spine. "There are more books, I see." He stepped to the side of the overturned table, gathered the other two volumes, and placed them together in a neat pile on the bar. All of the men continued to watch him as if his actions were highly significant.

"So—" he turned to face Muller. "We have established that there was a book, in fact, three books."

"What'd you want with that book, Helms?" Muller demanded.

He was met by a scowl. "Nothin'. I was jus' funnin'—like Ben said. Then them Rebs started playin' rough, an' we jus' gave 'em a lesson."

Fowler snorted. "I say Helms started it, an' th' jumpin' went th' other way 'round, Sergeant. An' that's all I got to say."

"Well, it isn't all I have to say! Sergeant, just what is going on here?"

Whoever, having once heard that turkey cock crow, could ever forget it, thought Drew. Captain Bayliss strode in, powdery white dust graying his blue blouse, his face redder and more sun peeled than ever. The troopers behind Muller stiffened into wooden soldiers, all expression vanishing from their features until they matched each other in exact anonymity.

"Sergeant, take those two men into custody." A jerk of the head indicated Drew and Anse. The Kentuckian straightened.

"On what charge, Captain?" he got out.

"Attacking a United States soldier."

"In performance of his duty, Captain?" Reese Topham cut in. "I hardly think you can say that. Your men were apparently off duty. At least they were in here, drinking, too. You *did* serve them, Fowler?"

"Sure did, boss! Let's see now. . . . Helms, he had whisky; so did Stevens. Mitchell, now, he had a beer——"

"It remains that they were attacked while wearing the uniform!" Bayliss' glare now included the full company before him.

"From what I've heard, they did the attacking," Topham pointed out. "At least Helms seems to have given provocation. No, Captain Bayliss, your men were in here drinking. They started a brawl. Your sergeant very rightly broke it up. That's the sum of the matter!"

Bayliss' high color was fading. "You want it left that way, Topham?" he asked icily. "This only confirms my contention that matters in Tubacca are completely out of control, that the Rebel element has the backing of the citizens. I shall so report it."

"That is your privilege." Topham nodded. "But this is still Tubacca and not your camp, Captain. And *my* cantina. If you want to declare my establishment out of bounds for your men, that is also your privilege."

"I do so—immediately! Sergeant, get these men out of here!"

"What about the prisoners, sir?"

"I think the captain will agree there are no prisoners," Topham said. "We would be obliged to give evidence at any army hearing, Captain. Kirby here is not a troublemaker. I would unhesitatingly vouch for him."

Bayliss looked directly at Drew.

"You have a job? A reason for being in town?" He shot the questions as he might have shot slugs from his Colt. Nye answered before Drew could.

"He sure has a job, Cap'n. He's ridin' th' rough string for Rennie. An' he came to town with them remounts you're buyin'. An' what Topham says is true, th' kid ain't no troublemaker. He's 'bout th' most peaceful hombre I ever rode with."

"Rider for Rennie, eh? I might have known!" Bayliss snapped. "And what about this one—he riding for Rennie, too?" He pointed to Anse.

"He's my cousin," Drew returned. "He just got into town."

"Another Rebel?"

Anse stood up. "If you mean was I with th' Confederate army, Yankee—I sure was, from Shiloh clean through. Got me this to prove it. Do you want to see?" From the inner band of his hat he brought out a much creased paper. "No, you don't!" He twitched the sheet away when Bayliss reached for it. "I'll jus' let Mister Topham read it. I want to keep it safe." He handed the paper to the gambler.

"Parole, Captain, signed and made out properly," Topham reported. "Dated in Tennessee for a prisoner of war—June, 1865. I hardly think you can claim this is one of Kitchell's men, if that is what you have in mind."

"No, but he'll be out of this town or he'll answer to me. Both of you—next time you step over the line, I'm taking you both in!" Bayliss spoke now to Nye. "I heard young Shannon was here, that you had him in tow and that he's seen Kitchell. I want to talk to him."

"He's over to th' doc's, an' Doc'll have th' say 'bout that, Cap'n," Nye replied. "Johnny took a pretty bad crease 'long-side his skull."

"He'll answer a few questions that badly need answering." Bayliss was already on his way to the door. Nye stepped back and let him pass. He grinned.

"Let him have it out with Doc. Ain't nobody runnin' a stampede over Doc Matthews, not even th' cap'n when he's got his tail up an' ready to hook sod with both horns. Only, lissen here, kid, maybe you'd better keep outta sight. Seems like a man who's waitin' to catch a fella makin' his boot mark in th' wrong pasture can sometimes do it."

"Nye's right," Topham agreed. "Bayliss can either catch you off guard or see you're provoked again into doing something he can rope you in for. I'd get back to the Range and stay there until things settle down a little and someone else takes the good captain's mind off you."

"What about Anse? You take him on, Nye?" Drew asked.

"I ain't got th' authority to hire, Kirby. But no reason why he can't go down th' trail with us. Old Man is always on lookout for a good rider. Soon as we see how Johnny's doin', we'll head south. I already sent Greyfeather back to tell the Old Man th' kid's hurt an' up here. Reese, what'd you think 'bout Bayliss? That he'll try to take over runnin' the town?"

"Might just," the gambler replied.

"*Could* he do it?"

"I hardly think so. What he's really out for is Hunt's hide. He doesn't want a powerful civilian ready to face up to him all the time. If he can discredit *Don* Cazar in this country, he figures he has it made."

Nye laughed shortly. "Lordy, what bottle did he suck out a dream like that? A lizard might jus' as well try to fight it out with a cougar an' think he hadda chance of winnin'. This here's th' Range, an' ain't nobody but th' Old Man runs th' Range! Bayliss, he's ridin' for a fall as will jar them big grinnin' teeth of his right outta his jaws!"

"Maybe, only there can be upsets." Topham looked thoughtful.

"What kind—and how?" Drew asked quickly.

Topham was playing with the three books, setting them up, putting them flat again. "Hunt didn't take sides during the war, but he did have Southern sympathies in part. After all, he was Texas-born. And Johnny joined Howard when they raised that Confederate troop here. He retreated with Sibley's force back east and fought through the rest of the war on the Southern side. Yes, Bayliss, given the right circumstances and a sympathetic listening ear in high circles, could make trouble for Rennie. Especially if the good captain had an incident on which to hang such a report."

"You kinda shoved him into that out-of-bounds order for th' Jacks, didn't you now?" Nye pushed his hat to the back of his head and lit a cigarillo.

"Muller and most of the boys can be counted on not to cause any more than the normal pay-night disturbances. But there're some . . . What *did* happen here today, Kirby?"

Drew told it straight and flat in as few words as possible. And Topham's face was sober when he had finished. The gambler brought the top book of the pile down on the bar with a thud.

"I don't like it!"

"Jus' ornery meanness, warn't it? There's always a few hombres in any outfit as tries to push when they gits a slug or two under their belts," Nye observed.

"True. Only Helms went out of his way this time. And I'd like to know what triggered him into it. I can understand some roughhousing on his part—Stevens, too—providing these boys were on the prod in the beginning. But this book business was too deliberate. Books—" He held up the volume he was still fingering. "Where'd these come from anyway, Kirby?"

Drew retailed the story he had heard from Stein. Nye walked over to look at the display of reading matter, his interest plainly aroused.

"Lutterfield brought 'em in, eh? Now that's somethin'. Trunk in a cave . . . Sounds like these might belong to one of them mine men—a super, maybe. They pulled out fast in '61, right after th' army left. Except for Hodges, an' th' Rebs threw him in jail after they took his business an' what cash he had on hand."

"Could be," Topham agreed. "But where they came from doesn't matter as much as why Helms chose to use them the way he did. However—and now I'm giving it to you straight, Kirby—this is once I'd follow Bayliss' orders. You and your cousin here had better make yourselves scarce."

"An' jus' why?" Anse demanded. "We ain't givin' you any double-tongue wag over this——"

"I'm not saying you are. I'm just saying that Bayliss and probably Helms—maybe others—will be waiting, just as the captain promised. You can be easily suckered into just such another fight. And they'd be smarter about it next time, so you won't have anyone to call their bluff in your favor. Once they get you into the camp stockade, it might be difficult to get you out. And this is something else, stranger, you went for your gun a few minutes ago. Kirby stopped you, but next time that could lead to real trouble."

"I can't see why—" Drew began.

"Well"—Anse was on the defensive—"a man can take jus' so much pushin', an' we had more'n that! Next time anybody lays his dirty hands on me, he's gonna know he's had him trouble, all right!"

"I don't mean that." Drew waved Anse's retort aside. "I don't see why we were jumped in the first place. Unless it was because we happened to be here at a time when they wanted to start trouble?" He made that into a question and looked to Topham for the answer.

"Could be," the gambler admitted.

"Only you're not sure?" Drew persisted.

"Could be you were handy and they had some kind of a hint to start a ruckus just to show there ain't any proper law here. Could be that they knew you ride for Hunt and that made you just the game they wanted."

"Helms's kinda dumb to play any cute game," Nye protested. "An' th' sarge, he's always been a good guy, I don't see him bitin' happy on any such backhand orders."

"Not orders, no. Captain Bayliss is still too army to give any such orders. Helms's always been a troublemaker; he wouldn't need much more than a suggestion or two of the right sort. Helms, Stevens, Danny Birke, and that kid Mitchell. You're right so far, Nye." Topham grinned. "Like as not, I'm imaginin' things—a greenhorn huntin' Apaches behind every bush. None of that crew has the brains to see anything beyond the tip of his nose. No, I guess we can take it that you were handy and they had too much red-eye on empty stomachs. Only, I mean it, Kirby, you walk soft and get back to the Range as quick as you can."

"That suits me," Drew agreed.

"Come on over an' let Doc take a look at that face of yours," Nye ordered. "You look like you came up behind a mule an' the critter did a mite of dancin' backwards! You come 'long, too," he extended the invitation to include Anse.

His face patched up after a fashion, Drew lay full length on the hay in his old place over Shadow's stall back at Kells' stable. Anse sat crosslegged beside him, the bruise now a black shadow on his jaw.

"Somethin' 'bout this show's bad, plain as a black saddle on a white hoss. Nobody could be fannin' a six-gun for you personal, Drew, 'less you had a run-in before with one of them Blue Bellies." The Texan paused and Drew shook his head, wincing at the pain from his numerous cuts and bruises.

Anse went on. "Some hombres are always on th' peck once they get likkered up, but them troopers weren't that deep. Looks to me now, thinkin' it over, they was out to make sod fly. Could be as they had trouble with some other riders an' we was handy an' looked peaceable enough to take easy. But I dunno. You know, a fella who's scouted an' hunted Injuns an' popped bush cattle, to say nothin' of toppin' wild ones what can look like a nice quiet little pony one minute an' have a belly full of bedsprings an' a sky touchin' back th' next—a fella who's had him all that kinda experience an' a saddlebag full of surprises in his time gits so he can smell a storm comin' 'fore th' first cloud shows. If we had the sense we shoulda been born with, we'd ride hell-to-thunder outta here now!"

"Anse"—Drew wriggled up on one elbow—"you do that. I ain't going to pull you into anything—"

"So," the Texan said, nodding, "you've been swallowin' down a whim-wham or two your ownself?"

"Yes, but every one of them could be only a shadow to scare a jackrabbit."

"Only you plan to go out an' spit in th' shadow's eye?"

"Guess so."

"Then there'll be two of us. Providin' Rennie can use him 'nother hand. You know, this might be interestin'. 'Member what they used to say in the army? Don't go borrowin' trouble nor try to cross a river till you git th' water lappin' at your boots."

9 ✳

"Times is gittin' better." Crow Fenner rode with one knee cocked up over the horn of his saddle, allowing Tar to drop into a pace at which he seemed to be actually sleep-walking. The wagon train was traveling slow, the wagons riding heavy in the ruts with their burden of northern goods heading south. But they were strung in good order and Drew, having seen the screen of outriders and Pima Scouts, thought that though they offered temptation, they were not to be easily taken by anything less than a small troop, very well armed and reckless.

"Yes, siree, this here's th' second time we made th' trip through without havin' to burn up a sight of gunpowder! Guess them army boys millin' around back an' forth across th' territory do some good, after all. Pretty soon there won't be no need for wearin' guns loose an' tryin' to grow eyes in th' back of yore skull!" But Fenner's own rifle still rode on guard across his knees, and Drew noted that the scout never broke a searching survey of the countryside.

"Gittin' downright civilized, eh?" Anse brought his mount up equal with the other two.

Fenner spat. "Now that thar I ain't cottonin' to none. Ride

'long without some Injun or *bandido* poppin' lead at m'back. Yep, that's what a man kin enjoy. But I ain't takin' to have maybe one o' them thar engine trains snortin' out dirty smoke an' sparks hereabouts. Took me a ride on one of them things onct—never again! Why a man wants to git hisself all stuck up with cinders an' cover territory faster than th' Good Lord ever intended him to travel—that's some stupid thinkin' I can't take to. A good hoss, maybe a wagon, does a man want to do some tradin' like *Don* Cazar—that's right enough. But them trains, they's pure pizen an' a full soppin' keg o' it!"

Drew looked about him. The road, rutted deep by the heavy wagons, curled southward. Those wheel tracks had first been cut almost a hundred years earlier when the Spaniards had set up their southwestern outposts. This country was far older than Kentucky, and with just as bloody a history of wars, raids, and battles. Kentucky had been tamed; trains did puff along through the Blue Grass and the mountains there. But here—he shook his head in answer to his own thoughts.

"Ain't nobody gonna try to run a railroad through here," Anse replied promptly. "First place, they're gonna be busy for a while back east puttin' up new ones for all them what were busted up in th' war. Our boys an' theirs, too, got real expert toward th' end—could heat up a rail an' tie a regular noose in it, were some tree handy to rope it 'round. Gonna take th' Yankees some doin' to git all them back into place." He laughed. "Drew, 'member that time we took them river steamers an' had us a real feed? Times when I was in that Yankee stockade eatin' th' swill they called rations I used to dream 'bout them pickles an' canned peaches an' crackers with long sweetin' poured on 'em!"

"Heard tell as you boys don't think th' war's clear over yet," Fenner observed. "Didn't you have yoreselves a ruckus with th' soldiers at th' Four Jacks?"

Drew's reminiscent smile faded. But he was not going to keep on protesting about the right or wrong of what happened back in town. The way Nye and Topham had hustled Anse and him out with the wagon train had made it seem as if they were in disgrace, and that rankled a lot. What was expected of them—that they should have let Helms pour it on—maybe serve as butts for a series of practical jokes without raising a finger in their own defense? On the other hand, the Kentuckian could see the sense behind Topham's arguments. If Bayliss wanted to use Drew's connection with the Range as a weapon in some scheme against Hunt Rennie, then Hunt Rennie's son was only too willing to clear out. Perhaps he should clear out even farther and head for California. Drew began to think about that. There was Sage. She couldn't hope to make such a trip for maybe six months. That would mean putting off traveling until next spring or early summer. But six months ... Of course, he *could* go now. *Don* Cazar would buy the foal and Shadow, too, and give him a fair price. That would be relinquishing a dream. No Spur R brand would ever be established here in Arizona. But sometimes dreams were priced too high. . . .

"You're mighty grim-mouthed," Anse commented, glancing at Drew sideways. "Thinkin' of trains runnin' through here git you down that far? Or else that roughenin' up you took in town still sit sour on your stomach?"

"Sits sour all right," Drew admitted. "Sits sourer to think we were suckered into it."

The scout glanced from one to the other of the young men.

"You think there's somethin' in all that talk Topham was givin' lip to?" Anse asked.

"Could be. Can't say as how I'd like to find out the truth. Look here, Fenner, we've heard a lot about Captain Bayliss wantin' to make trouble for *Don* Cazar. Does everybody believe that?"

"Everybody wot ain't blind, deef, or outta their natural-born wits," Fenner replied. "Bayliss come out here two years ago. 'Fore that, Major Kenny, he was in command between here an' Tucson. Had him an outpost right on th' edge o' th' Range. Him an' *Don* Cazar, they never talked no war, 'cept 'gainst Apaches an' th' *bandidos*. Was there a raid, th' major, he took out th' troops; and *Don* Cazar, he took out his riders an' th' Pimas. 'Tween 'em they give everybody wot wanted a spot of trouble all they could chew off an' a lot more'n they could swallow. Kept things quiet even if a man hadda rest his hand on his rifle 'bout twenty-four hours outta every day.

"But this here Bayliss—he's been like a mule with a burr under his tail ever since he hit th' territory. Wants to have th' say 'bout everything—includin' wot goes on at th' Range —which he ain't never goin' t' have as long as *Don* Cazar kin sit th' saddle an' ride. Back in '62 when th' Rebs came poundin' in here, they spoke soft an' nice to *Don* Cazar. They wanted him to back their play an' see 'em straight on to Californy. He was from Texas an' them Texas boys jus' naturally thought as how he'd saddle up an' ride right 'long wi' 'em. Only he said it loud an' clear—that such ruckusin' round only meant th' whole country here'd go to pot. When th' army pulled out, th' Apaches got it into their heads as how they finally licked us good an' proper an' this here was their country fur th' takin'. Nearly was, too.

"Then th' Rebs got up on their high horse an' said as how iffen *Don* Cazar warn't with 'em, then he was agin 'em, an' they would jus' move in on *him*. He tol' 'em to go ahead an' try. An' seein' as how they was only one company hereabouts—Howard's Rangers—they didn't try. That's when Johnny Shannon had his big bust-up with his pa an'—"

"His father!" Drew could not help that exclamation.

"Wal, *Don* Cazar ain't Johnny's real pa, o' course. But he shore thinks th' world an' all of Johnny, raising him up from a li'l cub. Johnny warn't more'n four o' thereabouts when *Don* Cazar went back to Texas an' got him. *Don* Cazar's been like a pa to Johnny since, an' a mighty good one, too. But when th' Rangers was round here in '62 Johnny—he had a big row an' run off to join 'em. Jus' a half-growed kid, not big 'nough to raise a good brush o' hair on his chin yet. When th' Yankee boys from Californy came marchin' in an' th' Rebs had to skedaddle—Johnny, he went with 'em. Didn't see Johnny round here agin till last fall when he came ridin' in lookin' mighty beat out an' down in th' mouth. But when th' Union men came, they was thinkin' th' same 'bout *Don* Cazar. Wanted him to jump right in an' swim 'longside o' them. But he said as how th' safety of his people was what was important. He was fightin' Apaches an' holdin' th' land, an' that was what meant th' most to his thinkin'. Then the Yankees did a lot of fancy cussin' out 'bout him, trying to make out that he was a Reb' cause Johnny lit off with th' Southerners.

"Till they began to discover nothin' much goes on round here lessen *Don* Cazar has a finger in th' pot. An' they had to swaller a lotta them hot an' hasty words—stuck heavy in quite a few craws, I reckon." Fenner grinned. "Only, th' *Don,* he's got agin him now a big list of little men who'd like to be big chiefs. Every once in a while they gits together an' makes war talk. Never quite got up guts 'nough to paint their faces an' hit th' trail, not yet. But did somebody like Bayliss look like he was beginnin' to make things move, then he'd have a lotta willin' hands to help him shove. Up to now Johnny's been their best bet at gittin' th' Range into trouble."

Drew turned his head to look Fenner in the eye. "Now you think we are!" He did not know why he uttered that as a challenge; the words just came out that way.

"Not any more'n any of us wot can be drawed into a fight in town. You keep away from Bayliss. He can't come huntin' you without tippin' his hand so wide he'd never be able to play agin. Hey, here comes somebody poundin' leather so hard he's gonna beat it right intuh th' ground!" Fenner pulled up Tar, flung up his hand to signal the wagons to a halt.

Dust rolled in a cloud with two or three riders at its center. They were pushing the pace all right. Drew jerked his carbine from its saddle boot, saw Anse beat him to that action by a scant second or two. But the newcomers were already drawing rein, bringing their foam-lathered horses to a pawing stop. A buckskin-clad man mounted on a powerful grulla gelding faced Fenner, his whole tense body and snapping eyes backing the demand he made:

"Where's Johnny?"

"Back at town, Rennie, at Doc's. He ain't bad. Got him a head crease wot knocked him silly for a bit. Doc says a day o' two in bed and then he kin come home."

"How did it happen?" That second question was as sharp as the first.

"Nobody's got it straight outta him yet. Army patrol

picked him up on th' road close to town—looked like he'd been footin' it quite a spell. An' by that time he didn't know wot he was doin'. Nye got him to Doc's an' they put him to bed. He ain't said much, 'cept Kitchell jumped him down Long Canyon way——"

"Kitchell!" Hunt Rennie repeated the name and nodded. "But . . . Long Canyon . . ." There was a shade of puzzlement in his voice. "All right, carry on, Crow. I'll try to get back to the Stronghold before you pull south—if Johnny's all right. Maybe I can bring him back with me."

The grulla made what was close to a standing leap into a gallop and Rennie flashed along the line of wagons in the opposite direction toward Tubacca. Fenner signaled once more and the train began the slower trip southward.

Drew sat watching the dust arise again as the trio of riders pounded away. He could no longer make out individual riders, just the rising dust. Rennie on his way to Johnny Shannon . . . What had Fenner said—"li'l cub . . . warn't more 'n four." Drew Rennie at four—hard to sort out one very early memory from another. There had been that time Uncle Murray had caught him down at the creek, making paper boats. How could a child that young know one kind of paper from another? But Hunt Rennie's son was judged to have torn up a letter with deliberate malice, not just taken paper found conveniently on the veranda. Was he four then, or even younger? But he could remember the punishment very vividly. And the time he'd run off to see the circus come into town, he and Shelly . . . Cousin Jeff, Cousin Merry, they had tried to beg him off from Grandfather's punishment that time, not that they had succeeded. Drew Rennie at four, at six, at twelve, at sixteen—riding out at night with Castleman's Company, weaving a path south through enemy-occupied territory to join General Morgan—few of those would-be cavalrymen over twenty-one. Yes, he could remember for Drew Rennie all the way back.

"Hey, you plannin' to claim this here range?" Anse's horse trotted up, and Drew was suddenly aware that the trailer of the last wagon had already pulled past him. He tightened rein, and the well-trained horse broke into a canter.

"Not hardly." He tried to meet Anse's attempt at humor halfway. "Don't look too promisin'."

"Lissen here"—Anse rode so close their spurs were near to hitting—"you sure you got hold of th' right end of th' runnin' iron now?"

"What do you mean?"

"Well, 'bout Shannon. You heard what Fenner said— Rennie's like a pa to him. An' maybe . . ." His voice died away.

"And maybe that's that? He has my place, and it's really his now?" Drew asked bleakly. "Could be."

Yes, it could well be that this was a good time to bow out. Maybe he should not have ridden out of Tubacca at all. Maybe he should have cut out of the game yesterday. . . . Or never come down into the valley weeks ago . . . or left Red Springs . . . Those "maybes" stretched as far back and as neatly in line as the railroad tracks they had been talking about earlier, one slipping smoothly into another as if cast in one strong string of doubts. Just as he had had that moment of disappointment the first time he had seen Hunt Rennie, so he felt that identical void now, only twice as wide and deep.

What had he expected, anyway? Some kind of instant recognition on his father's part? That all the welcoming would be on the other side, breaking right through the barrier he had been building for years? His feelings were so illogical he could have laughed at them, only he had no laughter left. He had not tried to open the door, so why did he care that it remained firmly shut?

"Did you ever think about California, Anse? Sounds like a place a man would like to see."

He was conscious that the Texan's horse quickened pace, only to be reined in again.

"You thinkin' about cuttin' out? Yesterday—"

"Yesterday—" Drew tried to think back to how he had felt yesterday about Topham's warning and how he himself had held the absurd belief that if *Don* Cazar was going to be in trouble, Drew himself wanted to be there. That was yesterday. But still he pointed his horse south—to the place where Hunt Rennie would return, bringing Johnny Shannon.

The Kentuckian fell back on the old "wait and see." He had learned long since that time took care of a lot of worries. Now he made himself grin at Anse.

"Was worryin' about wet feet before my boots were in the river again," he confessed.

"Don't let it git to be no habit," the Texan warned. "You try ridin' *with* th' bumps awhile, not agin them!"

"Agreed." Drew urged his horse on toward the front of the train where they wouldn't have to breathe the dust.

". . . m' cousin, Anson Kirby . . ." Drew made the introduction to Bartolomé Rivas. The wagons were forted up outside the Stronghold, a second square, smaller but almost as easily defended as the adobe walls. In two or three days the train would pull out again, starting the long trip down into Sonora.

Rivas surveyed Anse none too amicably, his gaze going from man to horse and its gear, then back to the Texan once more.

"You are Tejano," he said flatly. "From the Neusca—"

Anse showed no surpise at being so accurately identified.

"Been bush poppin'," he agreed, smiling.

"Not much cattle here," Rivas returned.

"Run hosses in th' San Sabe 'fore th' war." Anse's tone was offhand, he might have been discussing the weather.

"*Don* Cazar decides," Bartolomé said. "There is work at the corrals, but he will decide."

"Fair enough," Anse agreed. When Bartolomé had moved out of hearing, he added for Drew's benefit:

"I think it'd be 'no' if that hombre had th' sayin'. He plumb don't like my style."

"But Rennie does need men—guards for the wagon trains, riders—"

Anse shrugged as he off-saddled. "Will he want one as got into a brawl about his third day in town? Anyway, maybe I've a day or so to breathe full before he tells me to roll m' bed again, if he's goin' to."

During the next three days Drew made a new discovery. Just as he had fallen into an easy, working rhythm with Anse back in the army—so that on occasion their thoughts and actions matched without the need for speech—now they combined operations in the corrals. Drew's bare and painfully acquired competence with the rope was paired to the Texan's range training, while Anse's cruder and faster methods of "toppin' a wild one" were smoothed by Drew's more patient gentling process. Both of them were so absorbed by what they were doing that Tubacca and what might be going on there had no more immediate meaning than the words in the books which had ridden to the Strong-hold in Drew's saddlebags.

In the late afternoon of the third day the Kentuckian was walking a long-legged bay on a lead when León climbed to the top pole of the corral.

"The *patrón* comes," he announced.

Drew faced about. Two riders escorted at hardly more than a fast walk a buckboard in which were two other men. Drew caught a glimpse of a white bandage under the brim of the passenger's hat and knew that Johnny Shannon was coming home.

"Anse!" Drew raised a hand, suddenly knowing that his fingers were moving in the old scout signal of trouble ahead.

The Texan came across the corral. Drew's bay snorted, took a dance step or two to the right as if it had picked up sudden tension from the men.

"What's up?" Anse pushed back his hat, turned up a corner of his neckerchief, and swabbed the lower half of his sweating face.

"Rennie's back."

Drew watched León hurry to take the buckboard reins, watched Hunt Rennie give a hand to Johnny. Then he saw Shannon jerk away from that aid, walking stiffly toward Casa Grande while Rennie stood for an instant looking after the younger man before following him.

Croaker tossed his head so high his limber ear bobbed in the murky air. He brayed mournfully. Anse glanced at the mule's long melancholy face.

"That's th' way you think it's gonna be, Croaker? Well, maybe so . . . maybe so."

10 ❈

"THIS WAITIN'—" Anse sat cross-legged on the bunk next to Drew's, his thumb spinning the rowel of one spur. "I never did take kindly to waitin'. Is he or ain't he gonna sign me on?"

Drew, lying flat, stared up at the muslin-covered ceiling which years of dust had turned to yellow-brown. "You ought to be used to it by now—waitin', I mean. We had us plenty of it in the army."

"Only that was sorta different, not kinda personal like this here. We was sittin' round on our heels then, waitin' for some general to make up his mind as to where he was gonna throw some lead fast. This is waitin' to know if *we're* goin' to be throwed—out!"

"I heard California—" Drew began again.

"You've sure taken a shine to Californy lately," Anse commented. Under his fingers the rowel whirred. "At least you talk about it enough." He sounded irritated. "Looky here, Drew, if that's the way you really feel, why don't you go? I'm sayin' you don't feel that way, not by a long sight."

What if Drew answered with the exact truth, that he did not know how he felt?

Nye came in, trailed by three of the other Rennie riders.

"Johnny's got him a hoss-size headache an' maybe so a pair of burnt ears. Th' Old Man musta lit into him hot an' heavy, chewed him out good. I'd say they warn't even talkin' by th' time they pulled up here. Seems like th' kid got an idear to scout north, struck trace near th' Long Canyon, rode th' sign on his own an' was bushwacked. Guess whoever did it thought Johnny was wolf meat, jus' took his hoss an' left him there. You gotta give th' kid credit for havin' it in him. He kept on goin' after he came to some——Walked till that patrol picked him up. I'd say he sure had him a run of pure solid luck! There wasn't much pawin' an' bellerin' left in him when Muller's boys brought him to town. Been gittin' a little of it back, though, seems like. But maybe this here will learn him a little hoss sense—"

"It was Kitchell's men who shot him?" León wanted to know.

"Could be. Warn't no Apaches, that's for certain. No Injun would have jus' shot him down an' not made sure he was crow bait. Sure a fool thing to do, ridin' there alone. Anyway, th' Old Man'll stick him into bed here, an' I'll bet you Johnny ain't gonna ride out anywhere without an eye on him—not for a good long while."

"Long Canyon—" Perse Donally, one of the other Anglo riders, paused in shucking his shirt to look inquiringly over his shoulder. "That sure is off th' trail th' kid was supposed to be followin'. How come he ever drifted that far north from th' wells round, anyway?"

"You ask him." Nye sat down on a bunk, flipped his hat away, and lay back. "Sure feels good jus' to stretch out a mite," he observed. "Th' Old Man, he was movin' like he warn't on speakin' terms with th' law an' there was a sheriff behind every rock. Usually he's calm as a hoss trough on a mild day. Johnny gittin' his hair cut with a slug sure shook Rennie up some, almost as much as it shook Johnny. As for th' kid ridin' north—well, I'd say that was some more of his tryin' to make a real big brag. Maybe he thought he could run down Kitchell all by hisself. Which is jus' about as straight thinkin' as kickin' a loaded polecat on th' tail end. But Johnny's always been like that. Do it now, think 'bout it later. Got him into more scrapes 'n I can count me on both hands. Hope th' Old Man gives it to him this time, hot an' heavy, both barrels plumb center!"

"*Sí,* it is true that Juanito looks for trouble." Chino Herrera rolled a cornshuck cigarette with precise, delicate twists of his fingers. "He is *el chivato*—the young billy goat—that one. Ready to take on *el toro* himself and lock horns. Such a one learns from knocks, not from warning words. But he is yet a boy. Give him time."

"He'd better give himself some time," Nye announced. "Next time it may be in th' head, not 'longside it, that he gits his lead. See you got back in one piece, you two fightin' wildcats," Nye said, grinning at Drew and Anse. "Nothin' like tryin' to take on th' army—two to one—with th' army havin' th' advantage. That eye's fadin' good, Drew, only two colors now, ain't it?"

Drew grunted and Nye laughed. "Bet th' captain is as techy as a teased snake every time he thinks 'bout you two. Wanted to have you all corralled nice an' neat out to th' camp where he could use his hooks an' make at least three ride mounts outta you. I'd walk soft near him for a while, or you'll have about as much chance as hens amblin' into a coyote powwow."

"Don't look like they was so tough they had to sneak up

on th' dipper to take a drink, do they now?" Donally asked of the room at large.

"Don't never judge no hoss by his coat an' curryin'," Anse retorted.

"I don't, son. I never do," Nye replied. "As far as I'm concerned, you're both so wild they have to tie a foot up when they give you a haircut. Only, that sort of rep don't go down good with th' Old Man."

"We figured it might not," Drew agreed. Nye's warning was only another confirmation of Drew's fears. Topham, Nye, all the rest, had made it only too plain: no trouble on the Range and no troublemakers.

He gathered up clean underrigging, another shirt. If Rennie did order him up to the big house for firing, Drew was not going to meet him stinking of horse and sweat. In the stream back of the water corral there was a bathing place, and chilly as it was, Drew intended to take advantage of it.

"A mite cold, ain't it?" Anse demanded from the bank as Drew splashed vigorously to offset the chill. But the Texan was shucking boots and clothing in turn.

There were a lot of shadows this close to twilight. Lamps twinkled in the Stronghold. A horse nickered from the corrals, was answered from the barn. Then a bray—Croaker sounding off. From the hills came the far-off *yip-yip-yip* of a coyote.

"Hey!" Anse stood up knee-high in the water.

"What's the matter?" Drew called.

"Thought I saw somethin' movin' over there!"

Drew took a scrambling leap out of the water to their tangle of clothing, his hand reaching for one of the Colts in the belt he had left carefully on top of the pile. All those stories of Apaches weaseling into touching distance of the guard at the Stronghold . . . Why, only last year the younger Rivas boy had had his throat slit out in the hay field within sight of his home!

The Kentuckian crouched, alert, Anse beside him now, both listening for any suspicious sound. At last they huddled into their clothes, hurried back to the bunkhouse. Bartolomé was there waiting for them.

"You Tejanos—" There was no pretense of friendliness in his hail. "The *patrón* will see you, pronto!"

They went, tugging their clothing into order as they paused outside the door. Drew rapped, took the sound from within as an invitation, and pushed aside the heavy oak planks.

Outwardly the room was unchanged. No one had moved those old Spanish chests, the skin rugs, the table, since his last visit there. But he had the feeling that it was chill now, cold, as if a hearth fire had been allowed to die into ashes. Perhaps that thought crossed his mind because Hunt Rennie stood by the fireplace moving the toe of his boot back and forth across a smear of gray powder. His back greeted them unwelcomingly, and the silence lengthened uncomfortably until Drew did as he always had and met the unpleasant head-on.

"You wanted us, suh?" It was like being back in the army. Even his arm twitched as if some muscle was activated by memory to make one of those informal military salutes the scouts favored.

Hunt Rennie did turn now. His eyes leveled on them. In the light of the candles his cheeks looked even more hollow tonight, and he moved stiffly as might a man who was not only bone-tired in body, thought Drew, but weary in mind as well.

"You are Anson Kirby?" he addressed the Texan first.

"Yes, suh." Anse, too, must be caught up in the same web of memory. That was his old report-to-the-commanding-officer voice.

"I understand you two thought it necessary to take on some troopers in the Jacks."

What was the proper reply to that? Drew wondered. Probably it was best to follow the old army rule of keep the mouth shut, never volunteer, no explanations. If Hunt Rennie had had the story from Topham or Nye, he already knew how the fight began.

"I won't have troublemakers on the Range." Now the voice, too, was tired. The youthfulness which had impressed Drew on their initial meeting had drained from this man tonight. He was taut as if pulled harp-string tight inside. Drew knew that feeling also. But what battle had Rennie emerged from—some struggle with Shannon or Bayliss?

Then the words made sense, penetrating his concern for the man who had said them. Well, this dismissal only matched his gloomiest expectations.

"Can't any of you young fools get it through your thick heads that the war's over? Saloon brawling with the army ain't going to change that. It'll only get you into worse difficulties around here."

A spark of protest awoke inside Drew. Rennie was reading this all wrong. He and Anse certainly hadn't been trying to wipe away the bitter taste of Gainesville by jumping some blue coats in a cantina hundreds of miles and more than a year away from where they had been forced to admit, at last, that bulletless carbines and bare feet could not keep on shooting and marching.

"Must have been mistaken about you, Kirby." Now Rennie looked at Drew.

The Kentuckian met those dark eyes squarely, his first unvoiced protest stiffening into defiance. But he faced the older man steadily. Anse, watching them both, drew a small, fast breath. Good thing for Drew there were no other witnesses now; the likeness between the two Rennies was unmistakable at this moment.

Hunt Rennie did not follow up his half accusation. He appeared to be expecting some reply. What? A childish promise to be a good boy, not to do it again? Drew's half-unconscious concern for this man burned away speedily, ignited by what he deemed injustice.

Anse broke the too long silence. "I don't know what you heard 'bout that there fight, suh," he drawled. "Can't see as how we could have done no different nohow. But that's no call to saddle it all on Drew. Me, I had a hand—two fists—in it, too. An' if that's what's th' matter, I can pull out——"

"No!" Drew's hand came up in the old gesture to stop the line of march. "We'll both ride, Mr. Rennie. We don't aim to argue the matter any. Only—there's one thing—I brought Shadow and the filly down with the wagon train. The foal's too young to trail on now. They're blooded stock. I've papers for them. I'll sell. . . ."

He loathed saying every word of that. It was not only the thought of giving up Shadow and the foal, though he knew that would cut with a deeper hurt every day. It was having to ask any kind of favor from this man. Not that such a sale was a favor; Rennie ought to be glad to get such blood for the Range.

"You ain't goin' to do that!" Anse was stung into angry protest.

But Drew was unaware of the Texan's outburst, his entire attention for Hunt Rennie. The tall man came over to the table, moved one of the candelabra forward as if to throw more light on Drew.

"That your choice of solutions, boy—to run?"

Drew flushed. The unfairness of that jab pushed him off balance. What *did* this man want of him anyway? Rennie had said it plain that he did not want Drew and Anse on the Range.

"Running never settled anything." Rennie's fingers traced the spread of the candelabra's arms. "Neither does jumping to conclusions. Has anyone said you were through here, unless by your own choice?"

Drew was jarred into an answer. "You said—"

Rennie sighed. "Do any of you young fire-eaters ever listen to more than one tenth of what any of your elders say? I *am* saying and making it plain: If you make a steady practice of trading punches with a trooper or with any one else because you take a dislike to his face, the way his ears stick out, how he walks or talks, or what color coat he wore in the war, then you can roll your beds and ride out—the sooner the better.

"Reese Topham tells me that he explained the local situation to you, and you appeared to understand it then. Any difficulty with the army could have serious consequences, not just for you, but for the Range as well. This time you were not the aggressors. But after being forewarned, if it happens again, I'll be hard to convince that you were in the right. The war's over—keep on remembering that. This is new country where it doesn't, or shouldn't, matter whether a man wore a blue coat or marched under the Stars and Bars. You're far too young to let the past cut off the future. Wars can finish a whole way of life for a man. . . ." His eyes no longer held Drew's; he was looking beyond toward the half-open door or perhaps at something that he alone could see. "You have to learn to throw away broken things, not cherish them. Never look back!" That dry, tired voice took on a fierce intensity. Then he was back with them again.

"Two Kirbys riding for the same spread is going to be rather confusing. You are Drew, and you are Anson—Anson—" He repeated the name. "What part of Texas are you from?"

"Pa had him a spread down near th' San Sabe 'fore th' Comanches came. He was Anson, too—in th' Rangers for a while, Pa was."

"Tall man, with a lot of freckles and red hair? Best rider in Miggs' Company—" It was half question, half assertion.

"You knew Pa!" Anse shouldered past Drew. "That was Pa right enough. He rode with Lieutenant Miggs in the Mex War."

Hunt Rennie was smiling. Once more years spun away from him. "I ought to know him, son. He toted me across his saddle for a mighty long five miles on a blistering hot day, I having as much to say about the matter as a sack of corn, and being three times as heavy in spite of a starvation diet. Yes, I'll remember Anson Kirby. He and his squad were the first Americans I ran into after I broke out of a filthy prison. Funny though"—he glanced at Drew—"I don't remember his mentioning a brother. You *are* his nephew?"

Anse was quick to the rescue. "Pa—he an' Drew's Pa— they weren't too close. Drew's Pa was town folks. He sent Drew to Kaintuck for schoolin'. Pa, he favored th' range an' th' free land west—"

Rennie nodded. "Well, Anson, if you're as good a rider as your father, we can use you here. Horse knowledge seems to run in your family. Now, shortly we are expecting a *Coronel* Luis Oliveri who's to buy horses for the Juarez forces. He may need some assistance in driving them as far as the border. If he does, both of you'll go."

"Yes, suh."

Drew's agreement was drowned out by a harsh cry from overhead. Rennie went into action, so swiftly that for a startled moment Drew was left gaping at empty space. *Don* Cazar had caught up one of the rifles from under a window and had crossed the doorway to look back at the roof of the Casa Grande, calling out an inquiry in another language.

"Apaches don't attack at night!" Drew was heading for the door in turn.

"Outlaws do, when it pays," Anse shot out grimly.

But on a second hail from the rooftop sentry post Rennie swung the rifle over his arm and faced the outer gate of the patio.

"Unbar, Francisco!" he called in Spanish.

One leaf of the massive door folded back to allow in a small party of horsemen. One saddled but riderless mount galloped along with the rest. Another man held to the high horn with both hands and weaved back and forth while a comrade riding beside him strove to keep him from toppling to the ground. Drew had an impression of bright, almost gaudy uniforms. The men of the Stronghold poured out to take the horses, helping down more than one blood-stained soldier. Their leader, a slender man with dusty gold lace banding his high collar, came directly to Rennie.

"*Don* Cazar." His Spanish was a flood in which Drew was lost almost immediately, but Anse listened with parted lips and then translated a quick account.

"This here's th' *Coronel*. He an' his men was bush-whacked. Got away 'cause they met th' wagon train goin' south an' whoever was eatin' their dust huntin' them didn't seem to like the odds. Not Apaches, probably *bandidos*——"

"Kitchell?" Drew asked.

"My guess is they ain't sure. Got hit quick an' had to stampede to save their skins."

Oliveri's men were taken in and Drew saw Rennie him-self going from one of the wounded to another, applying bandages and once probing skillfully for a bullet. Drew commented on that, and Nye answered:

"Old Man knows what's he's doin'. He ain't no real doc, of course, but was I totin' me a hunka lead in some seri-ous part, I'd rather have him diggin' for it than a lotta docs I've seen out here. Heard tell as how once he was plannin' to be a real doc hisself. He sure can take care of a fella good. What I'd like to know is how them bushwhackers knew jus' where to lay down an' wait for Oliveri."

"What do you mean?"

"This here *Coronel,* he was comin' to buy hosses an' so he was carryin' money or else somethin' as could pass for money. We all knowed he was comin'. But we didn't know when or what road, an' he wasn't tellin' that his side of th' border neither. Only some jasper had such a good idea as to that what an' where, he an' some *amigos* was squattin' back of rocks jus' waitin' for th' *Coronel* to ride into their little pocket of fire."

"Mexicans could have trailed them up, cut ahead and waited—"

"Sure. Only this operation was too slick for most *bandidos*. They don't go in for timed, planned things; they jus' cut loose when they see a chance. This was different. Only Fenner an' some of the train guards ridin' in spoiled their game."

"Kitchell then?"

"Sounds more like. Don't think Kitchell's some common ridge-ridin' bad man. He'd never've lasted this long was that so—not with th' Old Man an' th' army an' what law there is in th' territory all gunnin' for him. Plans things, Kitchell does, an' so far his plannin' has always paid off.

"There's something else true now, too. Was Kitchell plannin' to make a break south, he'd want him a good big stake to cover him on cold nights an' winter days. I jus' wonder if this here ain't th' first of a lot of fancy raidin' jobs. Could be he'll hit fast an' hard, gather up all th' sweepin's an' light out. Could jus' be . . ."

"Don't promise us much shadin' times, does it?" Anse remarked. "Sounds like everybody's goin' to have to set up a string an' ride hosses in rotation. That is, always supposin' your supposin' is right."

"Yeah, always supposin' that," Nye agreed.

11 ✺

"Magnífico!"

Drew glanced over Shiloh's back to the speaker. *Coronel* Oliveri paused in the doorway of the stable to study the stallion with almost exuberant admiration mirrored on his dark and mobile features.

"*Don* Cazar"—the Mexican officer raised a gloved hand in a beckoning gesture—"*por favor,* Excellency . . . this one, he is of the Blood?"

Hunt Rennie joined Oliveri. "You are right. He is indeed of the Blood," he assented.

"It is past all hope then to offer for him?" Oliveri was smiling, but his eyes held a greedy glint Drew had seen before. Shiloh was apt to produce that reaction in any horseman.

"He is not mine to sell, *Coronel.* He belongs to *Señor* Kirby who stands there with him."

"So?" Oliveri's open astonishment irritated Drew. Maybe he did have on rough work clothes and look the part of a range drifter. But then when the *Coronel* had arrived here last night, *he* had not been too neat either.

"A fine horse, *señor.*" Oliveri came on in, now including Drew in his gaze.

"I think so, *Coronel,*" Drew returned shortly. He gave a last brush to flank and smoothed the saddle blanket.

"From a distance you have brought him, *señor?*" Oliveri walked about the stud as Drew went to fetch his saddle.

"From Kentucky." Was he unduly suspicious or was there a challenge in the Mexican officer's voice—a faint suggestion that the antecedents of both horse and owner were in question?

"Kentucky . . ." Oliveri stumbled in his repetition of the word. "I have heard of Kentucky horses."

"Most people have." Drew tightened the cinch. Then his pride in Shiloh banished some of his stiffness. "He is of the line of Eclipse." Maybe that would not mean much to a Mexican, though. The breeding of eastern American horses probably did not register south of the border.

"*Señor*—such a one—he is not for sale?"

"No." Drew knew that sounded curt, but Oliveri ruffled him. He added, "One does not sell a friend."

Oliveri gave what sounded to Drew like an exaggerated sigh. "*Señor,* you have spoiled my day. How can one look at lesser animals when one has seen such a treasure? *Don* Cazar, the Range harbors so many treasures—Oro, and now this one. How is he named, *señor?*"

"Shiloh."

"Shiloh . . ." The *Coronel* made a sibilant hiss of the word. "An Indio name?"

"No, a battle." Drew prepared to lead out. "In the war."

"So. And this one is a fighter, too. I think. *Señor,* should you ever wish to sell, *por favor,* remember one Luis Oliveri! For such a horse as this—*sí,* a man might give a fortune!

Ah, to ride into camp before that puffed-up gamecock of a Merinda on such a horse!" Oliveri closed his eyes as if better to imagine the triumph.

"Shiloh's not for sale, *Coronel*," Drew replied.

Oliveri shrugged. "Perhaps now, no. But time changes and chance changes, *señor*. So remember Luis Oliveri will give a fortune—and this is the truth, *señor!*"

"Hunt!" Drew was forced to halt as Johnny Shannon stood straight ahead of him in the stable entrance. "Teodoro Trinfan's come in with some news you oughta hear."

"So? Well. I'm coming. *Coronel,* Johnny can show you the stock we have ready. I will be back as soon as I can."

"Still I say"—Oliveri shook his head as Rennie pushed past Drew and Shiloh and went out—"that after seeing this one, all others will be as pale shadows of nothingness. But since I must have horses, *Señor* Shannon, I will look at horses. *Buenos días, señor.*" He raised a hand to Drew and the Kentuckian nodded.

But Shannon still stood in the doorway, and short of walking straight into him there was no way for Drew to leave. Johnny was smiling a little—just as he had back in Tubacca in Topham's office before the race.

"Seems like you've got you a four-legged gold mine there, Kirby," he said. "Better keep your eyes peeled—gold claims have been jumped before in this country. Kitchell'd give a lot to git a hoss like that to run south."

"He'd have to," Drew said grimly. "In lead—if he wanted it that way."

"Kinda sure of that, ain't you?" The smile had not cracked, nor had it reached those shuttered blue eyes. Why did everyone say Johnny Shannon was a boy? Inside he was older than most of the men Drew had known—as old and cold as the desert rocks in nighttime. Again the Kentuckian was teased by a scrap of memory. Once before he had seen old eyes in a boy's face, when it had meant deadly danger for him.

"When a man has somethin' as belongs to him, he doesn't step aside easy if another makes a play to grab it," he said.

For the first time then he did see a flicker in Shannon's eyes. And his hand tightened so on the reins that some fraction of his reaction must have reached Shiloh. The horse neighed, pawed with a forefoot.

"Jus' what I've always thought, too, Kirby." Shannon's voice was softer, more drawling than ever. And there was menace in it—but why? What did Shannon have against him? This was more now than the fact that they had both bristled, incompatible, at their first meeting. It was more than just instinctive dislike. No, Johnny Shannon was not a reckless boy; Drew Kirby knew that, if no one else on the Range did.

"*Coronel*"—Shannon stepped aside from the door—"we may not be able to git you somethin' as fine as this here prancer, but we ain't altogether lackin' in mighty good hosses. Come 'long an' look 'em over. . . ."

Drew rode off, out of the patio gate, giving Shiloh his daily workout, trying to guess what Johnny Shannon had against him. Had he been right in his fear that Johnny had not been unconscious back in Tubacca, that he had caught Anse's greeting? Rennie was not too common a name, but he did not see how Johnny could possibly have hit upon the truth.

What if he had, though? To Johnny, Drew could loom as a threat. He might be baffled as to why the Kentuckian had not made a move to claim kinship with Hunt. How much of Rennie's own past history was known to the people here? His escape from prison during the Mexican War was common knowledge. But, come to think of it, no one had mentioned his youthful marriage or the fact that he was a widower. Perhaps even Johnny had never heard that story, close to Hunt as he was. But Drew dared ask no questions.

He was still puzzling over the situation when he returned an hour later. Nye, Anse, and a couple of the other riders had some of the recently broken mounts out, showing them off to Oliveri. There was shouting, noise, and confusion around the corrals and Drew slipped past without pausing. He had finished with Shiloh and was on his way to the bunkhouse when Hunt Rennie hailed him.

"Drew!" An imperative wave of the hand brought him to join *Don* Cazar and to discover Anse already there, rolling his bed. For a second or two Drew blinked—the occupation fitted in too well with their worries of the night before. But Hunt Rennie was already explaining.

"Teodoro tells me that they've found traces of shod horses being driven back in the canyons. This late the grass is beginning to brown, but there are still some sections where stock can be wintered. I want to know more about this. Since both of you are newcomers—" Rennie paused and then added: "Your riding away from here might appear to others that you had quit, were joining up with the mustangers on your own."

"To hunt horses?" Drew asked.

"Not wild ones."

"Sounds like trouble." Anse tied his bedroll.

"In this country we expect trouble, from any direction— including up and down!" Rennie returned. "But I find it disturbing that broken stock is being herded back there. Such

maneuvers can mean only one thing—stolen animals are
being gathered for a run to the border. And some of them
could be army owned; a remount corral was raided just before I left town. I would not care, just now, to have any army
mounts located on this Range—no matter where they were
hidden or by whom. If they are there, I want to be the one
to find them and return them to the proper owners. It would
please certain parties to find stolen stock hereabouts—par-
ticularly army.

"Now"—he gave an order he obviously expected to be
obeyed—"if you do find anything, don't try to take over
yourselves. That's final. This is nothing to rush into just to
burn powder. And above all I want no mixing it up with
any army patrol riding south. Do you both understand?"

Drew nodded.

"Yes, suh," Anse replied promptly. "We jus' git high behind an' take care. What the mustangers got to do with
this?"

"Nothing. Except they can show you the tracks, and with
them you can cover a good part of the country in question.
There's been no Apache sign down there, and Running Fox
will accompany you—only not so openly as to be noticed."

"You think someone may be watchin' the Stronghold?"
Drew asked as he buckled his saddlebags.

"I don't know anything for sure. But a couple of incidents
lately have suggested that someone knows a lot more about
what's going on here than I like. It would be easy enough
to lie out in the hills and keep field glasses on us down here.
And when a man is familiar with the general routine of a
place, he can guess a sight too much and too close just by
watching the comings and goings. So—you're going to ride

out within the hour and be well along before you camp tonight. We can't waste time."

The nights were chill and the cold made them huddle turtle fashion into the upturned collars of their short riding coats and jam their hats down as far as possible on their heads. Winter breathed across the land now with the coming of dark.

They traveled at an angle, the pace set by Teodoro who led a pack mule. Somewhere out there in the dark the Pima Scout was prowling. But he had had his orders: no contact with the three travelers unless there was fear of attack. And both Anse and Drew were alert, knowing that the farther one went from the Stronghold the less one relaxed guard.

"Kinda nippy, ain't it?" Anse said. In the very dim light Drew could just make out that the Texan was holding his gloved hand to his mouth, puffing at the crooked fingers. "Ain't as bad as ridin' out a norther, though. I 'mind me how jus' 'fore th' war—I was ridin' for wages for Old Man Shaw then—we had a norther hit. I'm tellin' you, it was so cold th' ramrod came out to give th' mornin' orders an' his words, they jus' naturally froze up solid. Us boys, we hadda go git th' wood ax an' chop 'em apart 'fore we knew what we was all to do. Now that's what I call bein' cold!"

Drew laughed. "Don't think it ever gets quite that cold hereabouts."

It was good being away from the Stronghold, out here with Anse. It was as if he had been let out of lessons, or freed from a sense of duty and responsibility which was a growing burden.

"Nope. Texas sure is a lotta country, a whole bag with

odds an' ends stuffed in any which way. 'Course this is new range to me. But what I've seen of it, were you jus' able to run off th' *bandidos* an' git th' Apaches offen it for good— why, it might be a right respectable sorta territory. A man could carve hisself out a spread as he could brag on."

"You'd like it?"

Anse blew on his fingers again. "Maybe—all things bein' considered, as they say. I've heard tell as how all a man needs to start his own brand is a loose rope, a runnin' iron, an' th' guts to use them. It's been done, an' is bein' done all th' time. Only I don't think as how th' Old Man would take to havin' any such big-ideared neighbor here. Not much cattle, though, to interest a wide loop man. Now hosses— everyone says as how they's plenty of wild stuff. You got you Shiloh, Drew, an' you said you made a foal deal with th' Old Man. Git some more good-lookin' an' actin' wild ones an' you're in business—runnin' your Spur R brand. Three-four years, an' th' luck a man has always got to hope for, an' you've more'n jus' a stake—you've got roots an' a spread!"

"*We* have," Drew corrected. "Why'd you suppose I wanted that foal deal? There's free land to be had in the valley. Some of the ranchers cleared out when the Apaches started raidin' and they're not comin' back. We might look over what Trinfan has picked up as long as we are out here. I know the Old Man hasn't contracted for anything but gettin' rid of that Pinto stud. We could make an offer for any good slicks—put the Spur R on them and run them in on the Range. Rennie has already said that's all right with him."

"Whoee!" Anse muffled one of the old spirited war yells into a husky whisper. "You an' me, we're goin' to do it!

Ain't nobody can put hobbles on a pair of Tejanos as has their chewin' teeth fast on th' bit!"

It was something to think about, all right. But future chances should not take a man's mind off the job immediately ahead. Only tonight, out here, Drew had a feeling of being able to do anything—from touching the sky with his uplifted hand to fighting Kitchell man to man. That, however, was just what Hunt Rennie did *not* want and what Drew had promised not to do.

Horses to be found back in the rough country, hidden away in the maze of pocket canyons where there was water and enough browning grass to keep them from straying. There must be hundreds of places ready to be used that way. But how come Kitchell could hide out in Apache country? Nothing Drew knew of that tribe fitted in with the idea of a white outlaw band sharing their hunting ground unmolested. It had never mattered to an Apache whether a man rode on the north or south side of the law— if his skin was white, that automatically made him prey. Drew said so now.

Teodoro answered that. "Apaches want guns, *señor*. Their arrows are deadly, but guns are always better."

"I'd think," Anse cut in, "that any guns Kitchell'd have he'd be hangin' on to—needin' them his ownself. Can't be easy for *him* to git them, neither."

"Not here, no," Teodoro agreed. "But south, that is different. There is big trouble in Mexico—this French emperor fights Juarez, so there is much confusion. In wartime guns can be lost. A party of soldiers are cut off, as was *Coronel* Oliveri almost—men can be killed. But a gun—it is not buried with a man. A gun is still useful, worth money, if he who picks it up from beside the dead does not want it for himself. So—such a *bandido* as this Kitchell, he could take horses, good, trained horses—maybe from the army—and he would run them south. He would sell them for money, *sí,* probably much money. But also he could trade for guns—two, three, five guns at a time. Not as good as those his own men carry—old ones maybe, but good enough for Apaches. He would then bring these north, give them as payment for being left alone."

"Why wouldn't the Apaches just kill him and his men and grab what they have?" Drew pointed out what seemed to him the obvious flaw in the system.

"Apaches, they are not stupid. Guns they could take. But once such a gun is broken, where can they get another? They cannot walk into Tubacca or Tucson to buy what they need. Kitchell's men do, perhaps—it is thought that they do so. Also when he trades at the border it is with men who would meet the Apaches with fire and bullets. Apache war parties are never large. Perhaps in all this part of the country there are not more than half a hundred warriors—and those scattered in small bands. I do not say that this is truth, *Señor* Kirby. I only say that it would explain many things—such as why Kitchell has not been caught."

"Makes sense," Anse commented. "Always did hear as how Apaches were meaner'n snakes but they wasn't stupid. Keep a tame gunrunner to work for 'em—that sounds like th' tricky sorta play they cotton to. If it is so, th' man who gits Kitchell may jus' rid this country of some of them two-legged wolves into th' bargain."

"According to what I've heard," Drew said, "this Kitchell claims to lead a regular Confederate force that hasn't surrendered. If he wants to make that valid, he wouldn't dare any such deal!"

"I'll bet you without waitin' to see a hole card," Anse replied, "that if that coyote was ever ridin' on our side—which I don't stretch ear to—he cut loose them traces long ago. There were them buzzards we had us a coupla run-ins with back in Tennessee, 'member? Scum . . . some of 'em wearin' blue coats, some gray, but they was all jus' murderin' outlaws. What did they whine when they was caught? Did th' Yankees run 'em in, then they was unlucky Reb scouts. An' when our boys licked up a nest of th' varmints—why, we'd taken us a mess o' respectable Yank 'Irregulars,' 'cordin' to their story. 'Course none of their protestin' kept 'em from stretched necks." His hand went to his own. "I oughta know, seein' as how I was picked up with a parcel of 'em an' was close 'nough to feel th' wind when a noose swung by.

"This here Kitchell—I'm takin' Bible oath he's th' same mangy breed. Maybe so he started out to be Reb, but that was a long time ago an' he crossed over th' river long since. An' some of them beauties back east, they'da lapped muddy water outta an Apache's boot tracks, did it mean savin' their dirty hides. Sounds to me, Teodoro, like you've some plain, straightforward thinkin' there—a mighty interestin' idea. An' maybe we're jus' goin' to attend to th' provin' of it!"

"Not by ourselves," Drew corrected. "We have our orders."

"Sure. But there ain't no order ever given what says a man has to stand up an' be shot at an' he don't shoot back. No, I ain't sniffin' up trouble's hot trail like a bush hound. But neither am I goin' t' sit down an' fold my two hands together when trouble hits as it's like to do out here."

Drew agreed with that, though he did not say so. Rennie must know the circumstances. They would have to defend themselves if it came to a fight. But he could hope that, if Kitchell had stocked some hidden canyons with stolen horses, the outlaw leader had left no guards on duty thereabouts. With Running Fox prowling ahead and with him and Anse using all the scout tricks they had learned in wartime, they should be able to learn just how correct Teodoro's suspicions were.

12 ✻

"SEE, SEÑORES, THE LAND LIES SO. . . ." Hilario Trinfan's crooked body pulled together in a lopsided perch as he squatted range fashion beside the morning campfire. He had smoothed a space of ground the width of his two hands and was setting out twigs and stones to create a miniature relief map of the couuntryside. "Here is the water hole to which the Pinto comes. Above that we were—moving in from this side. To do so we crossed here." A black-rimmed nail stabbed into the dust.

"It is then we see the tracks—five ahead—all shod horses, but not ridden, save for one."

"Apaches could have been running them," Drew commented.

"No." Trinfan shook his head. "This far from pursuit the Apaches would not have moved so. The Indio, he eats horse-flesh. There would have been signs of a fire. Or one of the animals cut down. These horses were being moved with care—not pushed too hard. We trailed them on to here." Hilario stabbed his finger into the dust again. "Then—Teodoro, now tell them what you saw."

The younger mustanger hung over the crude map. "I

climbed, *señores,* up over the rocks. It is bad, that ground, high, steep—but with care one can reach a ledge. And along that one can go to look down into the next canyon. A good place for horses—there is water and grass. I stayed there watching with the glasses *Don* Cazar gave my father, the glasses which bring the far close. There were poles set up in the rocks through which they brought those horses— making it like a pen we build for wild ones. But those in it were not wild."

"How many—an' what brands?" Anse wanted to know.

Teodoro shrugged. "There are many trees, rocks; one can not see everywhere. I counted twenty head—there is room for more. As to brands, even the glasses could not make those plain to the eyes of one lying above. But there is no other ranchero who would run horses on the Range and *Don* Cazar's *manadas* are not driven in here—does he want the wild ones to run off his mares? Horses would be kept so for only one reason, that they must be hidden. And in such a place as we found they could be left for maybe a month, or more. *Don* Cazar's riders do not patrol this far away from the Stronghold. Had it not been that the Pinto causes so much trouble, even we would not be here."

"What about the Pinto? If he's all you say, wouldn't he try to get at this band?" asked Drew.

"No reason if they are saddle stock—no mares among them," Anse said thoughtfully. "But would those hombres who put 'em there jus' leave—no guards or nothin'?"

"That is what we do not know," Hilario replied. "We took every precaution against being seen when Teodoro climbed to look into the canyon. And—this I believe—we were not suspected if there was any watcher. Otherwise, otherwise, *señores,* we would not have been alive to greet you when you rode in last night! This Kitchell, he is like an Apache—here, there, everywhere. Today I am easier because you have brought the Pima, because we have two more guns in this camp."

"Why didn't you pull out yourselves?" Anse asked curiously.

"Because, were we watched, that would have made our discovery as plain as if we stood out in the open and shouted it to the winds. For three days before we found that trail we had been building a pen for wild ones, casting about for the tracks and runs of the Pinto's band. Having done so, we would not leave without completing our drive. And, should those out there suspect"—Trinfan shook his head—"we would not have lived to reach the Stronghold, and that is the truth."

"This is also truth, *padre.*" Faquita came to the fire and picked up the coffeepot, pouring the thick black liquid into the waiting line of tin cups. "It is time for us to finish and be on the move—not to just talk of what must be done."

Drew looked up in surprise. The girl was wearing breeches, ready to ride. In addition, instead of the gunbelts which all the men wore as a matter of course, Faquita had tucked a pair of derringers in the front of her sash belt. Their small grips showed above the faded silk folds.

"She goin' with us?" the Kentuckian asked, as the girl kicked dust over the campfire and stowed the empty pot in the cart. "Ain't that dangerous—for her?"

Hilario got to his feet with a lurch that made his crippled state only too plain. *"Señor,* to hunt the wild ones is dangerous. You see me, twisted like a root, no? Not tall and straight as a man should be. This was done by the wild ones—in one small moment when I was not quick enough. Among us—

the mustangers—it is often the daughters who are the best riders. They are quick, eager, riding lighter than their brothers or their fathers. And to some it is a loved life. With Faquita that is true. As for danger—is that not always with us?

"In war danger is a thing which one man makes for another. In this country the land itself fights man—war or no war. A cloudburst fills an arroyo with a flood without warning, and a man is drowned amidst desert sand where only hours before he could have died for lack of that same water. There is a fall of rocks, a fall of horse, a stampede of cattle, sickness which strikes at a lone traveler out of nowhere. Yet have you not ridden to war, and come now to live on this land? *Sí,* we have danger—but a man can also die in his bed in the midst of a village with strong walls. And to everyone his own way of life. Now we ride. . . ."

They did indeed ride, following a trail which, as far as Drew could see, existed only in the minds of the mustangers. But the three Mexicans swung along so confidently that he and Anse joined without question or argument.

At a distance they circled the waiting pen with walls of entwined brush and sapling, ready to funnel driven horses into a blind canyon. The Pinto's band must be located, somehow shaken out of the rocky territory their wily leader favored, before that drive could begin. Water, Trinfan said, would be the key. Horses must drink and they were creatures of habit, never ranging far from some one hole they had made their own. Trinfan blankets already flapped about the Pinto's chosen spring. They had seen the horses approach several times in the past two days and shy away from those flapping things with the fearsome man scent.

"As long as La Bruja is with them," Faquita said, coming up beside Drew, "they will not come."

"La Bruja?"

"The Witch, as Anglos would say. We call her so because of her cunning. She is the wise one who keeps lookout. I say she is possessed by the Evil One. It is possible the Pinto is her son. Together they have always outwitted the hunters. But La Bruja is old—she runs more stiffly. Last time in the chase she began to drop behind. She is of no use, only a nuisance. It is the White One I wish to drop rope over!"

"The White One?"

"*Sí*. She is Nieve—the snow of the upper mountains. Among our people you will hear many tales of white ones, without a dark spot on them—the Ghost Stallions that run the plains and no man may lay rope over. But this mare is the truth! And someday—" Her eyes shone and she seemed to be making some vow Drew would be called to bear witness to. "Someday she will be mine! Not to trail south and sell—no—but to keep, always!"

"She must be very beautiful," he commented.

"It is not only that, *señor*. You have a fine horse, one which beat *Don* Cazar's Oro, is that not so?"

"Yes. Shiloh . . ."

"And to you that one is above all other horses. If you lost him, you would be—like hungry . . . inside you, is that not also so?"

"Yes!" Her earnestness triggered that instant response from him.

"So it is with me since I have seen Nieve. Men find such a horse; for years they follow the band in which it runs to snare it. They will suffer broken bones, as did my father, and hunger, and thirst, because there is one tossing head, one set of flying heels before them. Sometimes they are lucky and they catch that one. If they do not, there is in them a pinch of winter even when the desert sun is hot. Once I loved all horses—now there is this one which I must have!"

"I hope you get her!"

"*Señor,* last season I hoped. This season—this season I have belief that my hopes will come true. Ah, look, the Indio!"

She pointed with quirt and Drew glanced left. He saw what appeared to be an outcrop of rock among many others move, then rise on sturdy legs to meet them.

Running Fox, a brown blanket twisted over one shoulder, the rest of him stripped down to breechclout and moccasins, padded up to Hilario Trinfan and spoke in the guttural Pima. The mustanger translated.

"The horses are still there. But there is a camp of two men on the north slope above the canyon. Both men are Anglos. They are armed with rifles and take turns watching."

"Can we reach a place from where we can read the brands on the horses?" Drew asked.

Trinfan questioned the Pima.

"*Sí.* But you can not go there by day. You must go in at dusk, wait out the night, and then see what you could in the early morning. Leave before sunup. Otherwise the watchers may be able to locate you. He says"—Trinfan smiled—"that *he* could go at high noon and would not be seen. But for a white man is a different matter."

"Waste a whole day jus' waitin'!" Anse protested.

"*Señor,* when one balances time against death, then I

would say time is the better choice," Hilario replied. "But this day will not be wasted. If any watch us—as well as those horses—they will see us about our business and will have no doubt that we hunt wild horses, not stolen ones."

So Drew and Anse joined the mustangers' hunting. To Anse this was something he had done before. Drew remembered that the Texan had been working with just such a hunting party when his family had been wiped out by the Comanches in '59. But to Drew it was a new experience and he was deeply intrigued by what he saw and the reasons for such action.

All they sighted of the Pinto's now thoroughly thirsty band was the stud himself and a black mare—La Bruja—looking down from a vantage point high on a rocky rim. And the hunters did not try to reach them, knowing that all the wild ones would be long gone before they could reach that lookout.

"This is the fourth day." Hilario Trinfan sat his buckskin at the water hole, watched Teodoro make careful adjustment of the blankets tied on the bushes. "They will be wild with thirst. Tomorrow the blankets will be taken down. There will be no sign of man here. By mid-afternoon the mares will be ready to fight past the Pinto for water. He can not hold them away. So, they will come and drink—too much. Perhaps he will come, too. If he does"—Trinfan snapped his fingers—"I shall be waiting with a rifle. We take no more chances with that one! Anyway, the mares will be heavy and slow with all the water in their bellies. They can be herded into our trap. Then he will come, *sí,* that one will come—no one can take his mares from him! He will be mad with rage, too angry to be any longer so cunning. We shall have him then. And there will be no more killings of studs here."

At dusk Running Fox slipped down to the camp, but not far enough into the circle of firelight to be sighted by any watcher in the night. Then with Drew and Anse he was off again.

Within less than a quarter-hour Drew could have laughed wryly at his past satisfaction in his prowess as a scout. Compared to this flitting shadow he was a bush bull crashing through the brush. Anse was better, much better, but even he was far below the standard set by the Pima. The trio climbed, crept, crouched for long moments waiting for Drew knew not what—some sound, some scent, some sight in the night which Running Fox would accept as assurance of temporary safety.

The Kentuckian had no idea of how long it took them to reach the perch into which they at last pushed. A breastwork of rock was before him; the half circle of a shallow cave cut off a portion of the star-pointed sky above. "Stay—here." The two words were grunted at them out of the dark. Then nothing . . . Running Fox had vanished in a way which could make a man believe they had been escorted not by a living Pima, but by a ghost from that long-forgotten race which had left their houses scattered in canyon niches up and down this country.

It was cold, even though the half cave shielded most of the wind. Drew unrolled the blanket he had carried tied about him, and he squeezed down beside Anse. Their combined body warmth ought to keep them fairly comfortable. Drew doubled his hands inside his coat, wriggling his gloved fingers to keep them from stiffening.

"Sure do wish there was some way a fella could bring him

a little invisible fire along on a trip like this," Anse commented. "Ain't goin' to be what I'd name right out as a comfortable night."

"Never seems to be any easy way to do a hard thing," Drew assented. He hugged himself, his hands slipped back and forth about his waist. Under his two shirts—he had added the second before he left the Stronghold—the band of his money belt made a lump and now his hands ran along it.

He had had no occasion to open any of those pockets since he had left Tubacca the first time. Now, to take his mind off immediate discomfort, he tried to estimate by touch alone how many coins still remained in the two pockets. The middle section of the three divisions held his papers. There were those for the horses, the parole he had brought from Gainesville, the two letters he had not been able to bring himself to deliver to Hunt Rennie. One was from Cousin Merry, and the other was a formal, close-to-legal statement drawn up by Uncle Forbes' attorney. Both were intended to prove the identity of one Drew Rennie beyond any reasonable doubt.

Drew's fingers stilled above that pocket. It felt too thick, bunchy under his pinching. Whatever—? He squirmed around, free of the blanket, and began to pull off his gloves.

"What's th' matter?" the Texan began in a whisper.

"Just a minute!" It was a clumsy business, pulling the belt free from under his layers of heavy clothing. But Drew got it across his knee. His chilled fingers picked at the fastening of the pocket. There was no packet of papers there— neither the sheets for the horse, nor the much-creased strip of the parole, nor the sealed envelope which had held both letters. Instead he plucked out what felt like shreds of grass and leaves, dry and crackling.

"What is it?" Anse leaned forward.

"My papers—they're gone!" Drew rummaged frantically, turning the pocket inside out. When—who?

"What papers, *compadre?*"

Drew explained.

"You've been wearin' that there belt constantly, ain't you?"

"Yes. Except—" He suddenly tensed. "That night, down by the swimmin' hole, when you thought you saw somethin' in the bushes . . . remember?"

"I remember. Looky here, who'd want 'em—an' why?"

"Shannon!" And in that moment Drew was as certain of that as if he had actually seen Johnny stripping them out of the belt.

"How'd he know you were carryin' anythin'?"

"He knew I had the belt. I left it with Topham when I raced Shiloh, and he saw me give it to him. And, Anse, he must have heard you call me 'Rennie' in the Jacks! If he did, he'd want to find out more—Rennie's not a common name. And Shannon's not stupid. He'd figure anything valuable I'd be carryin' would be in this belt."

"How come you didn't know it was gone?"

"I don't know. Seemed just as heavy and that pocket didn't ride any different when I had it on. No reason to open it lately."

"So—what's he got? Your hoss papers, your parole outta th' army, an' them two letters. Yeah, he's got jus' 'bout all he needs to make one big war smoke for you."

"And I can't prove he has them," Drew said bleakly.

"Jus' by makin' him one little private fire," Anse went

on, "he could about put you outta business, *compadre.*
There's only one thing to do."

"Such as?"

"Johnny Shannon has got to do some talkin' his ownself.
An' we can't wait too long to invite him to a chin-waggin'
party, neither!"

Anse was right. Shannon had only to slip that collection
of papers into the nearest fire and he would put an end to
Drew Rennie. Of course Drew could obtain duplicates of the
letters and horse papers from Kentucky, but that might take
months. And he did not know whether the parole could be
reissued from army records. Why, at this moment he could
not prove that he had served in the east with the Army of
Tennessee. Let Bayliss come down on him now and he was
defenseless. . . .

"We can't ride tonight," Anse added. "But come first
light we give a look-see here an' then we move—straight
back to th' Stronghold an' Shannon. Also—I'm sayin' this
'cause I think it's good advice, Drew. Now's th' time you've
got to go to th' Old Man an' tell him th' truth, quick as
you can. Sure, I know why you didn't want to claim kin
before, but now you'll have to."

Drew shook his head. "Not now—not with nothing to
back up my story. Shannon could give me the lie direct."

"I'm thinkin' you're showin' less brains than a dumb cow-
critter, *amigo.* But, lissen—I'm backin' your play. Does
Shannon cut up rough, he's got two of us hitchin' a holster
steady an' gittin' ready to loose lead."

"No, I'm not goin' to drag you in."

"Yeah—an' I mean yeah! We joined trails a long time
back, by that there mill pond in Kentucky, and we ain't
splittin' now. If a storm's walkin' up on us slow—or comin'

fast with its tail up—it's goin' to be both of us gittin' under or out together."

Drew put on the belt again. His impatience bit at him, but what Anse said made sense. They had been sent here to do a job and in the morning they would do it. Then they could ride back to the Stronghold. How he was going to handle Shannon he had no idea, but that he would have to he was sure.

The first light was a gray rim around the world as they lay flat, training the glasses Hilario had loaned them on two horses grazing not too far below.

"Well, that's it. U.S. As big an' plain as th' paint on a Comanche face an' almost as ugly. Them's army mounts an' I don't see no troopers hereabouts," Anse said.

Running Fox materialized in his ghostly fashion, and they retraced at a better speed and less effort the path which had brought them to the canyon perch. Just as they were about to top the ridge behind the mustanger camp, the Pima held up a warning hand.

"Long knives . . ."

"Troopers?" They went to their knees and made a stealthy crawl to the crest of the ridge.

There were troopers down there, all right. The Trinfans sat on their saddles while an officer walked up and down before them. Running Fox put a finger on Drew's arm and motioned to the left. The horses of the mustangers were browsing in a small dell, their night hobbles unloosed. Together the trio moved in that direction.

The Pima slipped ahead with a speed and efficiency of motion his companions envied. He had the two nearest horses in hand, leading them toward the bushes.

"Looks like we ride bareback." Anse caught at a hackamore, then mounted.

"Move!" Drew waved Running Fox to the other horse. "We can't wait to get another horse. You ride for the Stronghold, make it straight to Rennie and report. I'm stayin' here. I can say we were fired and Trinfan took me on as a hand."

Anse was the better rider under these circumstances, and the better scout. To wait to pick up a third horse was folly.

"What about Shannon?"

"Shannon'll have to wait!" Drew slapped the Texan's horse. It reared and then pounded off. Drew turned to walk back to the camp. He rounded the end of the ridge and stopped short. The round and deadly mouth of an Army Colt was pointed straight at his middle, covering the disastrously empty pocket of his money belt.

13 ✳

A LANTERN provided a very small and smoky light on a table of three boards mounted on boxes. If the furniture was makeshift, the walls of the room were not. Logs and adobe were just as effective for the purpose of confinement as stone blocks. Drew sat up on a bunk shell of board holding straw, and rested his head between his hands. He could follow the action which had brought him here, trace it back almost minute by minute over the past three days. How he had come here was plain enough; why was another matter.

Lieutenant Spath, back in the mustangers' camp, might have accepted the Kentuckian's story. Or he might at least have been uncertain enough not to arrest him, if only Trooper Stevens had not been one of the patrol. Once before Stevens had been most vocal about Rebs who were too free with their fists. Spath's trooper guard, reporting the escape of Running Fox and Anse, had condemned his captive fully as far as the lieutenant was concerned. The troopers had then searched their prisoner and to them a loaded money belt worn by a drifter did not make good sense, either—unless too much sense on the wrong side of the ledger. Drearily Drew had to admit that had he stood in the lieutenant's boots, he would have made exactly the same decision and brought his prisoner back to the camp.

So here he was now—just where Bayliss had promised to see him—in an army detention cell, with no proof of identity and the circumstantial evidence against him piling up by the minute. All they needed was some definite proof to tie him to Kitchell and he was lost. He had to pin his hopes on Anse—and *Don* Cazar.

Drew ground his boot heel into the dirt floor. That was just what he had sworn he would never do—call upon Hunt Rennie for help. Especially now, since the troopers had discovered those army-branded horses back in the canyon and Bayliss would try to use that against Rennie. Anse's escape had been a short-sighted solution, Drew knew. To the captain such action only tied the Range in deeper. The Kentuckian ran his fingers through his hair, trying to think of something which had *not* gone wrong.

The plank door banged open and Drew's head came up with a snap. No use letting these Yankees think they had him worried. The lantern, feeble as it was, picked out the stripes on the blouse of the first man, the tin plate in the hands of the second.

Drew looked down at the plate as it was slid under the bars and across the floor of his cell.

"Stew, Sergeant? Ain't that overfeedin'? Thought bread and water was more the captain's style for Reb prisoners." Drew was pleased that he was able to sound unconcerned.

"Cocky one, ain't you?" asked the man who had brought in the plate. "All you Rebs is alike—never know when you're licked—"

"Get along, Farley, that's enough," Muller broke in.

Drew picked up the plate and forced himself to spoon up

its contents. The stuff was still warm and not too bad. After the second spoonful he discovered that he was hungry—that much he would not have to pretend.

"Kid!"

Sergeant Muller's bulk shut most of the lantern glow out of the cell.

"You young squirts're all alike—never take no advice. But I'm gonna give it, anyway. When th' cap'n sees you, you button your lip! He ain't one as takes kindly to no smart talkin', 'specially not from a prisoner. As far as he's concerned he's got you about dead to rights—hoss thievin' from th' army."

"I'd like to know what proof he has," Drew returned sharply. "Your patrol picked me up well away from those horses—in the mustanger camp where I was workin'—and Captain Bayliss can't prove that's not true, either. Anyway, what difference does it make to you, Sergeant?"

"Since you ask, I don't rightly know, kid. Maybe you was spoilin' for a fight in th' Jacks an' did push our boys—"

"But you don't think so, Sergeant." Drew put the plate on the bunk and stood up to approach the bars. Muller was the taller; the Kentuckian had to raise his eyes to meet the sergeant's. The trooper's face was mostly in the shadow, but it was plain the man did not mean him any ill.

"I got m' reasons." Muller did not make any straighter answer. "But you think o' what th' cap'n does know about you, kid. You go ridin' 'round with gold on you—more money than any drifter ever sees in ten years or more. You're caught near where some stolen army stock is stashed away, an' your partner lights out hell-for-leather, breaking through army lines. An' we only got your story as to who you really are. I ask you—does that read good in the lieutenant's report when th' cap'n gets it?"

"No," Drew answered. "But what do you suggest doin' about it, Sergeant?"

"Got anybody in town as will speak up for you, Kirby? Reese Topham? He did before."

"He doesn't know any more than what he said right then. Trouble is, Sergeant, anybody I could ask to back me up I'd have to bring out from Kentucky—and I don't believe Captain Bayliss would wait for that."

"You work for Rennie, don't you?"

"Hunt Rennie has nothing to do with this. He didn't know those horses were on the Range—"

"Because you put them there, Kirby?"

Muller made a lightning about-face. He snapped to attention facing the captain.

"And what are you doing here, Sergeant?"

"Prisoner bein' fed, sir!" Muller reported stolidly.

"And there is no need for conversation. Dismissed, Sergeant!"

The captain watched Muller leave before he turned once more to Drew. "Kirby, do you know the penalty for horse stealing in this country?" he snapped.

"Yes."

"Then you must know just what you have to face."

"Captain . . ." Drew began slowly, wanting to make his words just right. There was no reason to let Bayliss think he could simply ride right over his prisoner. On the other hand Muller's advice had been good; it would be dangerous to antagonize the officer. "I had nothing to do with those stolen horses. We found them, yes, but they were already in the canyon. And there were two men guardin' them—up on the ridge. They must have cleared out when your patrol rode in, but they were there the night before."

"You saw them?"

"No, our scout did."

"What scout—that Indian who got away with your partner? I heard rumors that Kitchell had links with bronco Apaches, but I didn't believe any white man could stoop so low."

"That Indian"—Drew felt as if he were walking a very narrow mountain ledge in the dark, with a drop straight down to the middle of the world on one side—"was a Pima, one of the Stronghold scouts."

"So—Hunt Rennie *did* know about those horses!" Bayliss pounced.

"He did not! He sent us to the mustanger camp with a message, and the Pima rode scout for us. It's a regular order on the Range—take one of the Pimas if you are goin' any distance from where you can fort up. You can find out that's true easily enough." Drew was striving to keep a reasonable tone, to find an answer which *must* pierce through Bayliss' rancor. After all, Bayliss could not have held his present rank and station so long and been all hot-headed plunger.

"What was this so-important message Rennie had to have delivered to a camp of Mex mustangers?" Bayliss bored in. Even in the lantern's restricted light Drew could see the flush darkening the other's face.

"They are havin' trouble with a wild stud—a killer. Mr. Rennie wants him killed, quick. He sent the two of us out to help—thought with more hands it could be done."

"Kirby!" Bayliss' fists were on his hips, his head pushed forward from his shoulders until his sun-peeled face was only inches away from the bars between them. "Do I look like a stupid man, a man to be fed stories? You ride into town on a blooded stud, with a mare of like breeding, and a belt loaded down with gold. You give out that you served with Forrest—Forrest, a looting guerrilla and a murdering butcher! You've heard of Fort Pillow, Kirby? That's what decent men remember when anyone says 'Forrest' in their hearing! Only you can't even prove you were one of that gang of raiders, either, can you? Now I'll tell you just who and what you are.

"You're one of Kitchell's scavengers, come into town with gold for supplies and a chance to contact the people you want to meet. I've known for a long time that Topham, Rennie, and probably a dozen other so-called citizens of that miserable outlaws' roost are backing Kitchell. Now here's a chance to prove it!"

"Not through me, you don't," Drew cut in. "I'm just what I said I was from the beginnin', Captain. And you can't prove anything different."

"I don't have to prove it; you've convicted yourself, Kirby. You can't account for the gold you're carrying. And, if you rode with Forrest, where's your parole? You know you were told to carry it. I can deal with you just as any horse thief is dealt with. Why, I'll wager you can't even prove ownership of those horses you brought with you. Where're your sale papers? On the other hand, Kirby, if you do give us the evidence we need against Kitchell and those who are helping him, then the court might be moved to leniency. How old are you? Nineteen—twenty—? Rather young to hang."

"Captain, I can prove everything I've told you. In Kentucky I have kin. They can—"

"Kentucky!" Bayliss snorted. "Kentucky is far away, Kirby. Do you expect us to sit around waiting for some mythical kin of yours to appear from Kentucky with another set of lies to open this door?" He pounded with one fist against the cell portal. "I'm a reasonable man, Kirby, and I'm not asking too much—you know that. What're Kitchell, Rennie, Topham to you that you're willing to face a noose for them?"

"Kitchell I know nothin' about—except what I've heard and that's not good." Drew sat down on the bunk, partly because the chill which had crept down his back had poured into his legs and they felt oddly weak under him. "Reese Topham and Mr. Rennie—as far as I'm concerned they're honest men. I don't think, Captain, that you can prove I'm not, either."

"There is such a thing as over-confidence, Kirby, and it always comes to the fore in your kind!" Bayliss returned. "But after you do some serious thinking I believe you'll begin to see that this is one time you're not going to be able to lie or ride yourself out!"

He left without a backward glance. Drew picked up the plate, pushed the spoon back and forth through the congealing mess left on it. He could not choke down another mouthful. Just how much power did Bayliss have? Could he try a civilian by court-martial and get away with it? And to whom could Drew possibly appeal? Topham? Rennie? Apparently Bayliss wanted them enough to suggest Drew testify against them. Did he actually believe Drew guilty, or had that been a subtle invitation to perjury? The Kentuckian set the plate on the floor and got up again to make a minute study of the cell. His thought now was that maybe his only chance would be to break out.

But his first appraisal of the detention quarters had been

the right one. Given a pickax and a shovel, and an uninter-
rupted period of, say, a week, he might be able to tunnel
under one of the log walls. But otherwise he could not see
any other way of getting free—save to walk out through the
cell door. Drew threw himself on the bunk and tried to
think logically and clearly, but his tired body won over his
mind and he slept.

"Hey, you! Kirby, wake up! There's someone here to see
you!"

Drew reached for a Colt which was no longer under his
pillow and then rolled over and sat up groggily, rubbing one
hand across his smarting eyes. The lantern light had given
way to dusty sunshine, one bar of which now caught him
straight across the face.

"All right, Kirby, suppose you tell me what this is all
about!"

Drew's head came up, his hand fell. Hunt Rennie and
Lieutenant Spath stood side by side beyond the bars. Or
rather, not Hunt Rennie, but *Don* Cazar was there—for the
owner of the Range was wearing the formal Spanish dress
in which Drew had first seen him. And his expression was
one of withdrawal.

"They think that I'm one of Kitchell's men and that I had
something to do with those stolen horses we found on the
Range." He blurted it out badly.

"They also showed me about six hundred dollars in gold
found on you," Rennie returned. "I thought you needed a
job. You told Topham that, didn't you?"

"Yes, suh." Drew's bewilderment grew stronger. Hunt
Rennie sounded as if he believed part of Bayliss' accusation!

"That money's rightfully mine," Drew added.

"You can prove it?"

"Sure. Back in Kentucky . . ." Drew paused. Back-in-Kentucky proof would not help him here and now in Arizona.

"Kentucky?" Rennie's withdrawal appeared to increase by a score of miles. "I understood you were from Texas."

"Told you, Rennie," the lieutenant said, "his story doesn't hold together at all. A couple of really good questions and it falls right apart."

"I came here from Texas." Drew took stiff hold of himself. He was walking that narrow ledge again, and with a wind ready to push him off into a bottomless gulf. "Rode with a wagon train as far as Santa Fe—from there on with military supply wagons to Tucson. I was in Kentucky after the war; went home with a boy from my scout company. . . ."

"Who gave you two blooded horses and a belt full of gold for a good-by present?" scoffed Spath.

"Have you any proof of what you say closer than Kentucky?" Rennie ignored the lieutenant's aside. "I can account for your time on the Range, or most of it. But you'll have to answer for this money and where you came from originally. What about your surrender parole? I know you did have papers for the horses—Callie saw them. Produce those . . ."

"I can't." Drew's hands balled into fists where they rested on his knees.

"Sure you can't—you never had any!" Spath returned.

"I had them. I don't have them now." What was the use of trying to tell Rennie about his suspicions of Shannon? And if Johnny had destroyed the papers as well he might have, Drew could never make them believe him, anyway.

"Kirby, this is serious!" said Rennie. "You ride in from nowhere with two fine horses wearing a brand you say is your own. You have more money than any drifter ever carries. You claim to be a Texan, and yet now you say all the proof of your identity is in Kentucky. And—you are not Anson Kirby's cousin, are you?" That last question was shot out so suddenly that Drew answered before he thought.

"No."

"I thought so." Hunt Rennie nodded. "Education is a polisher, but I don't think three or four years' schooling would have made a Texas range rider ask for sherry over whisky—except to experiment with an exotic beverage. There were other things, too, which did not fit with the Kirby background once Anson turned up. Just who are you?"

Drew shrugged. "That doesn't matter now—as the lieutenant and Captain Bayliss have pointed out—if my only proof is in Kentucky and out of reach."

"I suppose you have heard of telegraphs?" Rennie's sarcasm was cold. "Communication with Kentucky is not so impossible as you appear to think. You give me a name and address —or names and addresses—and I'll do the rest. All you have to do is substantiate background and your army service, proving no possible contact with Kitchell. Then the captain will be forced to admit a mistake."

Give Hunt Rennie the name of Cousin Meredith Barrett, of Aunt Marianna's husband, Major Forbes—the addresses of Red Springs or Oak Hill? Drew could not while there was a chance that Anse might find the papers or make Johnny Shannon admit taking them. The Kentuckian could *not* tell Hunt Rennie who he was here and now.

"I want to talk to Anse," he said out of his own thoughts. "I've got to talk to Anse!"

"He's gone." Rennie's two words did not make sense at first. When they did, Drew jumped up and caught at the bars.

"Gone? Where?"

"Cleared out—got clean away." Again Spath supplied the information. "Or so they tell us. He went back to the Stronghold after he broke through our lines. But when a patrol rode down to get him, he was gone."

"Why?" Drew asked. "Why pick him up?"

"Why? Because he's in this, too!" Spath retorted. "Probably rode straight to Kitchell's hideout. Now, Mr. Rennie, time's up. The captain authorized this visit because he thought you might just get something out of the prisoner. Well, you did: an admission he's been passing under a false name. We know *what* he is—a renegade horse thief."

Drew was no longer completely aware of either man. But, as Rennie turned away, he broke through the mist of confusion which seemed to be enclosing him more tightly than the walls of the cell.

"Shannon. Where's Shannon?"

Hunt Rennie's head swung around. "What about Johnny?" he demanded.

"He took my papers—out of my belt!" This was probably the worst thing he could do, to accuse Johnny Shannon without proof.

"What papers, and why should he want them?" If Rennie had been remote before, now he was as chill as the Texas northers Anse had joked about.

"The parole, the horse papers, some letters . . ."

"You saw him take them? You know why he should want them?"

Drew shook his head once. He could not answer the second question now.

"Then how do you know Johnny took them?"

How did he know? Drew could give no sane reason for his conviction that it had been Johnny's fingers which had looted the pocket of papers and stuffed leaves and grass in their place.

"You'll have to do better than that, kid!" Spath laughed. "You must have known Shannon was gone, too. By the time he's back from Mexico he won't need to prove that's a lie."

Drew disregarded the lieutenant's comments—Rennie was the one who mattered. And in that moment the Kentuckian knew that he had made a fatal mistake. Why hadn't he agreed to telegraph Kentucky? Now there was no hope. As far as *Don* Cazar was concerned, one Drew Kirby could be written off the list. Drew had made an enemy of the very person he most wanted to convince. The Kentuckian swung around and walked to the one small, barred window through which he could see the sun. He walked blindly, trying not to hear those spurred boots moving out of the door . . . going away. . . .

14 ✳

THREE GOOD STRIDES one way, four another to measure the cell. Morning sun, gone by noon, daylight outside the window becoming dusk in turn. They fed him army rations, delivered under guard. And the guard never spoke. There was no use asking questions, and Drew had none left to ask, anyway. Except, by the morning of the second day after Rennie's visit, his wonder grew. Why was Bayliss delaying a formal charge against him? This wait could mean that the captain was not finding it so easy to prove he really did have a "renegade horse thief" in custody. But Drew knew he must pin no hopes on a thread that fine.

What had happened to Anse? And Shannon—gone to Mexico? He must have ridden back with the *Coronel*. Drew could expect nothing more from Rennie, or Topham. The Trinfans? Spath had marched them back, too, along with his prisoner, but the lieutenant had not had them under arrest. The mustangers were well known in this district and could prove their reason for being where they were found. And Kitchell had raided one of their corrals last season, so they had no possible tie with the elusive outlaw. Probably by now the Trinfans had returned to their hunt for the Pinto.

No, there was no use thinking that anyone was going to get him out of this—no one but himself, and he had bungled badly so far. Drew, his body tired with pacing the small cell, flung himself down on the bunk and listened to the sounds of the camp. He had pretty well worked out the routine by those sounds. The camp itself was a makeshift affair. Its core, of which this cell was a part, was an old ranch building. There were tents and a few lean-tos, on a plateau bounded on the east by a ravine, on the west by a creek bottom. Huts of stone, rawhide, and planks served as officers' quarters. In fact it was no more a fort than the bivouacs he had known during the war. Unfortunately this room was the most substantial part.

If he could only get out, and pick up his horses, then perhaps he could head for Mexico. There was a war on down there; a soldier could find an anonymous refuge in a foreign army. Shelby's whole Confederate command had crossed the Rio Grande to do just that. That part was easy. To get out of here—that was what he could not accomplish.

Two men always came together when they fed him, and they didn't open the cell door, but just pushed the plate through. A sentry was on duty outside. Drew could beat time to the sound of those footfalls day and night. And suppose he did get free of the cell; he would have to have a horse, supplies, arms. . . .

Drew rolled over on the cot and buried his face on his folded arms. He might as well try to get out of here by using will power alone to turn locks! They left the lantern burning all night to keep a light on him, and the sentry looked in the peephole every time he passed.

The Kentuckian did not know just when it was that he became conscious of the noise overhead. Lizards—maybe even rats—could move about the beams, hidden by the age-browned manta strips. But surely this was too late in the season for a lizard to be so lively by night when the temperature dropped with the rapidity of a weight plunging earthward. And rats aloft . . .

Drew did not change his position on the bunk, but his body tensed. No rat would stay in one place, gnawing with such purpose and concentration at a spot in the darkest corner of the cell roof. Anse? How or why the Texan could be at work there, Drew did not know. But that there was a stealthy attempt being made to reach him from above he was now sure.

His teeth closed on his wrist as he lay listening, to that scratching above, to the regular advance and retreat of the sentry. He heard the man pause by the door and knew he was under inspection. Well, let the Yankee look! He would see his prisoner peacefully sleeping.

Now the trooper was moving on, the noise above became sharper. There was a slight crackle. The linen roofing sagged under a burden, and Drew caught his breath in a gasp. Miraculously the yellow cloth supported the object—a bulge as big as a saddlebag. A portion of the roof which had given way?

The scratching, which had stilled, began again. Then the bulge was gone, pulled away from above. Dust sprinkled down from the disturbed manta. In the next instant Drew moved.

Using his hands on either side of his body, he raked up the straw which filled the box bunk. In a swift moment, timed to the sentry's passing to the farthest point from the spy hole, the Kentuckian rolled to the floor, slapped and pulled the blanket into place over the mounded straw. Not too good—it certainly would not fool any inspection within the room. But in the lantern light and this far from the door, the improvised dummy might satisfy the glance of the sentry for some precious seconds.

Drew was across the cell, flattened against the wall under the still quivering strip of material. More bulges appeared and disappeared, fragments fallen and retrieved. Then a sharp point pierced downward, the tip of a knife slitting the tough stuff. A slash, and the manta peeled back against the wall of the cell.

"*Señor—?*" It was so faint a whisper Drew hardly caught it.

"Yes!" He looked up with desperate eagerness into what he had hoped to see—the dark splotch of a hole.

A rawhide lariat smoothly braided, oiled into supple silkiness, dangled through. Drew got his hands on it, pulled it back against the wall as the sentry returned. He held his breath during that pause beside the spy hole, a pause which lengthened alarmingly. Then his body jerked in answer to a sound a half second before he realized what manner of sound. The sentry had sneezed. He sniffled, too, loudly; then he went on to complete his beat. The blanket and the straw—they had worked!

Drew pulled at the lariat, was answered by a return jerk. He jumped and began to climb. Then, with a wrench he was through the hole, other hands helping to pull.

"Come—pronto!" The hands were pushing, urging. He wriggled forward. Teodoro Trinfan! But why?

There was no time to ask; Drew could only obey directions. They made a worm's progress along the full length of the old ranch building, and dropped the lariat for a ladder to the ground. They crossed the small part of the camp near the ravine with the same caution they had used on the roof.

"*Señor* . . ." Teodoro's lips were at Drew's ear as the boy pressed against him in a thin cover of shadow. "Left—a big stone—put your hands on it—swing about and down."

Drew had to take that on blind trust. He had no idea what kind of a drop waited below, and only by firm will power did he follow orders. But his boot soles met a solid surface. Then he was caught about the waist and Hilario's voice whispered to him.

"*Señor,* you stand—so." Hands fumbled about him, looping him with a supporting lariat. "Now—we go! Your hand, *señor.*" Drew's left hand was caught in a tight grip which pulled him to the right, face to the wall. So secured, he inched along what he knew must be the face of the ravine, his toes on some small ledge midway between lip and foot.

Somehow the three of them reached ground level, their diagonal course of descent putting some distance between them and the camp. In spite of the cold of the night, Drew was wet with sweat as they threaded through heady sage brush. Now came the scent of horses, the sound of a hoof stamped impatiently on gravel.

"Trinfan?"

Topham! Here?

"*Si.*"

At Hilario's hissed assent, a figure detached itself from the utter black of the bushes and moved forward into a sliver of moonlight.

"You got him?"

"I'm here, if that's what you mean!" Drew answered for himself.

"And you'll be gone, soon," the gambler replied. "But there's one thing I have to know, Kirby. Were you telling the truth to Rennie—do you believe Johnny took your papers?"

What had that to do with the matter at hand? Drew wondered. But from the urgency of the demand he knew it did mean a great deal to Topham.

"Yes, I'm sure. But I can't prove it—unless I find them with him. He may have destroyed them already." Drew put into words the black foreboding which had ridden him for days.

"Why? What do they mean to him?"

Evasions and lies had gotten him into this mess; now he would see what stark truth would do.

"Because there were two letters—proof I'm Drew Rennie."

"Rennie?" Topham repeated. In the light Drew could not see his expression, but his voice was that of a completely baffled man. "Rennie?"

"I'm Hunt Rennie's son." There, he had said it—and nothing startling happened. Well, what had he expected— a clap of thunder, a bolt of lightning, the sudden appearance of a cavalry patrol across the nearest hilltop?

"So that's it!" Topham said slowly. "And Shannon suspected? But why the mystery? And—"

Drew took the questions in turn. "Shannon was at the Jacks when I met Anse. I thought he was unconscious, but he probably wasn't. Anse called me by my right name. As for why—my father doesn't know I'm alive. He was told I died at birth, along with my mother. They told *me* he was killed in the Mexican War before I was born. It was all because of an old family feud—too long a story to tell now. I've only known for about a year I had a father here in Arizona . . . but to make a claim on him, after all these years. . . . Maybe you don't understand why I didn't want to." He was telling it badly, but he'd been a fool about this from the start.

"Understand . . . yes, I think I can. There's a certain strain of bull-headed independence common to Rennies—I've met it head-on several times myself. And your choice was your own to make. But this . . . yes, it is just the move Shannon would make, given suspicion to push him into action. And now it may be pushing him even farther."

Drew was a little bewildered by Topham's ready acceptance of his story without any proof. But the tone of the last remark caught his full attention.

"What d' you mean? What's happened now?"

"I've had suspicions, pretty nasty ones, for some time. But I had your trouble—no proof. In the last three days I've picked up and sorted out a few very wild cards, and now they make a pat hand. Kitchell has had his contact hereabouts, all right, just as Bayliss has always insisted."

"You can't mean Shannon!"

"Johnny Shannon. And if he's doing what I think he is . . ." Topham paused. When he continued he had changed the subject. "Last night Nye rode up from the Range. Said that Kitchell made a raid, almost a clean sweep. Among other stock he gathered up was that prize stud of yours."

"Shiloh!"

And Shannon had the horse papers! The Kentuckian was thinking fast now.

"Yes, if Shannon *is* riding with Kitchell, now he can prove ownership of that stud and sell him anywhere without trouble." Topham could have been reading Drew's mind. "But that's not as important as something else. Hunt went hell-bent-for-leather out of here. He'll gather up that private army of his and try to trail the raiders. Maybe Kitchell will ride south, or maybe he'll head directly back into Apache country. Either way that trail's going to be as easy for anyone after him as walking barefoot through a good roaring fire! Hunt still has blind faith in Johnny . . . I was hoping you could help break that."

"That why you got me out of the camp?" Drew asked.

"Partly. Hunt told me what you said about Johnny taking your papers. I had you sized up as being too smart to make a claim like that unless you really believed it. And I thought maybe you could prove it, given a chance. If you can get to Hunt now . . . tell him the real truth before Johnny rigs something of a double-cross. . . ."

"Would he believe me any more than he did when I accused Shannon?" Drew asked bleakly. "I'll head south, all right. Nobody's goin' to lift Shiloh and get away with it as long as I'm able to fork a saddle and push. But if you're countin' on my bein' able to influence my—my father"—he stumbled over the word awkwardly—"don't!"

"I'm counting on nothing," Topham returned. "Just hoping now. For a long time we've heard about Johnny Shannon being a young hothead who found it hard to settle down after the war. I think there are two Johnnys and we are just beginning to know the real one. You could be his prime target now."

"Fair of you to point that out." Drew thought that at last he had found a real motive for Topham's services. "I'm likely to be bait, ain't that the truth of it?"

"If you are, the trap is going to be there. But now . . . get away from here. Teodoro will ride with you as guide."

"And the army after me. That's it!" Drew had mounted. "That's what you want, isn't it? Me to pull the troops south?

Huntin' down an escaped horse thief they might slam into Kitchell. . . ."

What a trick! Topham had planned it without asking Drew's support. But it called for enough audacity, luck, and nerve to be appealing. During the war the Kentuckian had seen such schemes win out time and time again.

"Why ain't Bayliss already ridin'?" he asked. "Hasn't he heard about the raid?"

"He's been heard to say a man can raid his own stock as a cover-up."

"What's wrong with him? Is he deaf, dumb, and blind!"

"No, just prejudiced and ridden by envy until he's not able to think straight any more. But he'll track you and follow quick enough!"

"He sure will. All right . . . we ride."

They did, Drew depending on the younger Trinfan's guidance. And, while Teodoro set a meandering trail, it was not one which a determined pursuer would have too much trouble following, come sunup or whenever that sentry discovered he was guarding a straw prisoner.

Once when they pulled up to breathe their horses, dismounting to loose cinches and cool the backs of the mounts, Drew indulged his curiosity further.

"How come you knew just where to make that hole to let me out?"

Teodoro laughed. "That was easy, *señor*. That was the Garza Rancho—only six months has the army been there. Many times we have camped within its walls when we brought in the best of the wild catch for sale. I know those buildings very well. When *Señor* Topham tells my father what must be done, we could plan well and quickly. I have heard what you said to *Señor* Topham, that you are the son of *Don* Cazar. Why did he not know of this? Why have you never lived here with him?"

"He didn't know I was alive, and I didn't know that he was. My grandfather—my mother's father—he hated *Don* Cazar very much, because of a duel and other things. So my father took my mother away secretly, brought her to Texas when they were both very young. Then *Don* Cazar went to war and the news came that he had been killed. My grandfather went to Texas and took my mother home with him. She died a few months later, when I was born.

"It was only after my grandfather died, two years ago, that letters from my father were found among his private papers. These I discovered when I came home from the war, learning that my father was alive and here in Arizona. Only we were strangers . . . I did not know whether he would like me for a son, or whether I wanted a stranger for a father. So, when I came here I took the name of my *compadre,* my friend from the war, Anse Kirby. I wanted to know my father before I made my claims."

"And *Señor* Juanito—for this he will hate you!"

"Because I did not tell who I was at the start?" Drew asked.

"No—because you are truly *Don* Cazar's son. Always *Don* Cazar, he treated *Señor* Juanito as a son, but I do not think that was enough. *Señor* Juanito, he is one who must have everything, all. Even when he was a boy, he was like that. Bartolomé Rivas, he braids beautiful ropes, and he made one for Juanito. Always I wanted a rope like that. I would watch Juanito use it and wish. Then once we spend Christmas at the Stronghold . . . it was after my father was hurt and *Don* Cazar had us to stay there so he could tend my father's wounds. Had *he* been with us when the wild ones stampeded, my father would not walk crooked, but we got him back to the ranch too late. But that is not what I would say. It was Christmas and *Don* Cazar gave to me a rope like that of Juanito, a fine rope which felt as if it was a part of a man's own arm when he swung it. Two days later, that rope, it was gone, never did I find it. But I knew—I had seen Juanito watching me when I tried that fine rope. And I knew his thoughts: no one must have a rope as good as Juanito's! Not long after that he ran away, to join the army. But really that was because *Don* Cazar caught him beating one of the Indios. Only that is not generally known. The Indio was being taught by *Don* Cazar to have charge of the grain storage, and Juanito thought that Indios are as dirt—should have no place among Anglos. *Señor* Juanito would hate with a black hate anyone who had a right to be a son at the Stronghold, a better right than he could claim. He must always be on top, at the head. Sometimes it would seem that he would, if he could, push aside *Don* Cazar himself. . . . Now I think we should ride again."

By dawn Drew had no idea where they were except that they pushed south. Whether they were now on the Range he did not know. And how in the immensity of this hostile country, they could fulfill Topham's hopes and lead the troop patrol to Rennie's posse, was something the Kentuckian did not even try to answer. The border lay south. If Kitchell had made such a sweeping raid, he would be certain to run the animals in that direction, for the outlaw was fully aware of Rennie's reputation and temper, and knew that *Don* Cazar would trail him with set determination.

This meant the outlaw must have set up some plan for avoiding pursuit. Rouse the Apaches? Or prepare an ambush? Either could work. Then Bayliss' men could be a saving factor. If the Kentuckian could locate Rennie, and ride in to his camp—or skulk close enough to it—that should bring the troops down.

But where was Anse? The Texan had not simply cleared out because of imminent trouble, Drew was sure of that. Had he followed Shannon to Mexico? This was one time when Drew could well understand the exasperation and frustration felt by an officer whose scouts did not report in as ordered and who had no idea of the disposition of reinforcements. Talk about going into something blind! But still he rode at a steady, mile-covering pace southward.

15 ❈

"STILL SOUTH . . ." Teodoro pointed out the hoof prints deep in the soft earth beside the water hole. Drew steadied himself with one hand on the stirrup leathers as he stooped to see more clearly. He was groggy with lack of sleep and felt that if he once allowed himself to slip completely to ground level, he would not get up again.

"Rennie's riders?"

Teodoro was on one knee, conning the mass of tracks as if they were a printed page. *"Sí*—there is the mark of Bartolomé Rivas' horse. It has a misshapen hoof; the shoe must always be well fitted."

"How far are they ahead now?" Drew had come to depend upon the young mustanger's judgment. Teodoro apparently was close to a Pima in his ability to read trace.

"Two hours—maybe three. But they will be at the pass and there they will stay."

"Why?"

"I think they will lay a trap for the raiders. There has been no sign that they trail now behind driven horses. *Don* Cazar does not pursue; he rides to cut off the road to Mexico. Kitchell's men, they would not take the open Sonora trail, that is folly for them. So they travel one ridden by men with a price on their heads. If Kitchell now moves south to stay, he will have with him all that he can carry, and he must come this way."

"If he hasn't gone already!"

"There is no sign," Teodoro repeated stubbornly.

"So we keep on ahead." Drew got down on both knees, splashed the muddy water-hole liquid into his face in an effort to clear his head.

They had changed mounts twice since leaving the camp, both times at the water forts on the Range. And the second time they had chanced three hours' sleep and a hot meal. But the rest of the time it was ride, chew on jerky and cold tortillas, and depend on Teodoro's sense of direction to take them eventually to their goal—the outlaws' gate into Mexico. Drew had long since stopped looking over his shoulder for any thundering advance of cavalry. If Bayliss was hunting the fugitives, he was not pushing the pace too hard.

"Not ahead, no." Teodoro drank from his cupped hand. "We go so . . ." He sketched a gesture east.

"Why?"

"It is never well to be shot by one's friends." The mustanger achieved a half smile, stretching the skin of his gaunt young face. "Always it is better to see before being seen."

When they started he led the way to the left at a walk. Drew, aroused now, looked about him carefully. This was rough country cut by pinnacles of red and yellow rock, backed by the purple ridges of the greater heights. It was desert land, too. They had long since left the abundance of the valley behind them. Here was the stiff angularity of cactus, the twisted vegetation of an arid land.

The crack of a carbine shattered the empty silence. Drew

pulled on reins as a second shot dug up a spurt of dust just beyond Teodoro's mount.

"Hold it! Right there."

That disembodied voice could have come from anywhere, but Drew thought it was from above and behind. Someone, holed up in the rocks, had them as perfect targets. The Kentuckian did not try to turn his head; there was no use giving the sharpshooter an excuse.

"All right, you . . . ." The voice was hollow, its timbre distorted by echo. "Throw off your guns an' git down . . . one at a time . . . th' Mex first."

Drew watched Teodoro slide out of the saddle.

"Stand away from that hoss . . . easy now."

The mustanger obeyed.

"Now you . . . do jus' like him."

Drew followed instructions carefully.

"Hands up—high! Now turn around."

They turned. A figure had detached itself from among the rocks they had passed moments earlier and came down toward them carbine ready.

"Anse!" Drew stumbled toward the Texan. The other's hat was gone. A torn shirt sleeve flapped about his left arm, allowing sight of a neckerchief knotted about his forearm. His coat trailed from one shoulder. "What in the world happened to you?"

Anse sat down suddenly on one of the boulders, his gaze on Drew. He shook his head slowly.

"I ain't seein' things," he said. "That's you, ain't it? Say— got any water?" His tongue curled over cracked lips.

Drew snatched the canteen from his saddle and hurried forward. More than a bloodstained bandage marked Anse, he could see now. He waited while the other seized the canteen avidly and drank. Then the Texan was smiling at him.

"Seems as how we's always meetin' up, don't it now? Likewise it's always to m' benefit, too. Only this time I've got me somethin' to trade. You keep on goin' down this trail, *compadre,* an' maybe you'll wind up with a spade pattin' you down nice an' smooth."

"What happened?"

Anse drank again with the discipline of a plains rider, a mouthful at a time.

"What didn't would be more like it, *amigo.* Yesterday, well, they got m' hoss—tried to git me. Only left their mark, though," Anse said, regarding his arm ruefully. "I've been wearin' off boot heels hoofin' it ever since. Tryin' to make it back to that there water hole."

"Who shot your horse?"

"I didn't see no name printed big 'cross his jacket, but I'm thinkin' it was Shannon."

"You were in Mexico?"

Anse shook his head. "No, an' Shannon ain't there, neither. I trailed along—ridin' th' high lines careful—when he went with that there Mex *Coronel* an' his men. Stayed with him 'bout a day, Shannon did. Then another man, Anglo, rode into their camp—had him a chin fest with Shannon, an' Johnny saddled up pronto, beat it with th' stranger. Thought he might be headin' home, but he weren't. So I kept on ridin' into their dust an' waitin' to find out what it was all 'bout.

"Shannon an' this hombre, they hit it up a pretty good lick till they got well away from th' Sonora trail. Then they skimmed it down till you'd think they had all month an' a handful of extra Sundays to git wherever they was goin'. Plumb wore me down amblin' 'long th' way they did. I sure 'nough 'bout scraped off my hoss's hoofs cuttin' down his speed.

"Spent a whole day jus' loungin' 'round in one camp. I'd say they was waitin' for someone—only nobody ever showed. So they went on, me followin'. I'll tell you one thing. This new hombre Shannon took up with, he was a real hard case. A short trigger man if I ever laid eye on one. Anyway we jus' kept on, with me tryin' to think iffen I should Injun up to git th' drop on 'em or not. Seemed to me, though, as how it might be brighter to kinda jus' drift their way an' see what's makin' 'em rattle their hocks out in th' middle of nowhere.

"Guess I weren't as smart as I thought I was. As I said, yesterday suddenly they give th' spurs an' lit out. Me, guess I got kinda upset 'bout losin' 'em an' followed a bit too hasty. Hoss came down with a hole in him. Me, I took another. Gave 'em a good sight of a man plugged where it means th' most an' that musta convinced 'em I wasn't no problem no more. So—that was what happened. I jus' pulled as green a trick as a sod-buster tryin' to crawl a wild one! An' where Shannon is now I don't know—only I don't think it's in Mexico."

"Probably with Kitchell." Hurriedly Drew filled in his own experiences and what he had learned from Topham.

Anse looked about him. "For territory what looks so bare," he commented, "this stretch of country sure must have a sight of population wanderin' 'round in it. Th' Old Man an' his posse somewheres up ahead, an' Shannon an' that side-kick of his, an' Kitchell maybe, as well as th' Yankees hotfootin' it behind you—or so you hope. Lordy, this's gonna be th' Battle of Nashville over again' do they all meet up! All we need is a coupla bull pups up on one of them ridges an' we could blow 'em all to hell-an'-gone! Jus' which bunch is goin' to claim us first?"

"*Señores,* that is already decided," Teodoro said quietly.

Drew looked up. Where had they come from, those four? Out of the rocks themselves? He only knew that now they were there, rifles over their forearms, ready to swing sights on the three below. His heart gave a lurch—Apaches? And then on the far right he recognized Greyfeather, Rennie's chief scout. And it was Greyfeather who pointed to them and to the way ahead, who gave an emphatic wave of the hand which was an order. Leading their horses, they obeyed, the Pimas falling in behind.

The back-door route to the pass was a rough one. They had to leave the horses and climb, two of the Pimas always in sight behind, guns ready. Anse sighed.

"Seems like we have lots of luck—all of it plain bad. These Injuns run us in an' as far as th' Old Man's concerned we're jus' what everybody claims we is. We're a coupla saddle bums as is only on th' loose 'cause we got up earlier an' owned faster hosses than th' sheriff! How'd we ever git our saddles slipped 'round so wrong, anyway?"

"I did it," Drew said bitterly. "It's not any of your doin', Anse. Tied myself up in a string of lies and now they have me tight. So help me, Anse, if I ever get this unsnarled, I'm never goin' to open my mouth again to say more'n 'yes' or 'no'!"

The Texan laughed. "You ain't never been one to color up a story redder'n a Navajo blanket! An' don't take on th' whole pack of this when only 'bout th' salt bag is of your buyin'. You ain't responsible for Kitchell, nor Johnny Shannon, nor Bayliss' wantin' to down th' Old Man. Can't see as how much of this is your doin', after all."

Rennie had set his ambush at the pass with care. At first sight there was no evidence of men lying in wait, but from the heights over which the Pimas brought their charges, Drew caught glimpses of men crouched behind sheltering rocks. The bulk of the Range posse was gathered in a hollow on the south side of the pass and it was there that Greyfeather delivered his catch.

Don Cazar surveyed them almost without interest. "Bayliss released you then," he said to Drew.

"No. Reese Topham and the Trinfans broke me out." Drew kept to his recent vow of truth-telling. And, he noticed with a spark of something approaching satisfaction, the truth seemed able to shake Rennie a little.

"Reese Topham broke you out! Why?" The demand was quick and to the point.

"He wanted me to play fox for the army's hounds . . . bring the troopers south . . . here," Drew replied. "Bayliss wouldn't march out and Topham thought that you needed some support—with Kitchell apparently on the move." Telling the truth did not mean you had to tell all of it. There was no reason to bring Shannon into this now and antagonize Rennie all over again.

"He what—?" His father was staring at him now with pure amazement. "But that doesn't make sense," he added as if to himself.

"No? I think it does, suh. Kitchell wouldn't have dared to raid the Range if he were goin' to stay in this country, would he? And after such a raid he'd head south. You believe that much or you wouldn't be here waitin' for him now. Nobody knows how many men ride with that gang—and maybe he can pull in the Apaches, too. They wouldn't pass up a good chance to get back at you. You have the reputation of being about the only white man in this territory to make them turn tail and give up a fight. Now—supposin' you do get Kitchell stopped here at the pass—and the army patrol comes in behind him. Then together you can finish him, and perhaps some bronco Apaches into the bargain. It could work."

Drew paused and then went on. "Of course, I have a good reason of my own for being here, apart from not wantin' to swallow Captain Bayliss' brand of justice. Kitchell's men took Shiloh. And nobody, nobody at all, suh, is goin' to run off that horse—not while I'm able to do something about it!"

"Seems to me, suh," Anse cut in now, "that three more guns is gonna be healthy for you to have 'round here, does th' fight work out th' way it can. Me, I don't make no big brag on my shootin'—but I never did wear no six-gun, nor tote no carbine, jus' for show."

"Of course, if you think we're Kitchell's plants," Drew added, "then keep us under guard. Only we're not and never were."

"Topham, Topham planned this?" Rennie still showed surprise. "I don't—"

A bird called flutingly. Rennie stiffened. Men moved, up slope, into cover, without direction.

"You two . . . get up there, behind those pointed rocks," *Don* Cazar directed with a stab of his finger. "I'll be right behind you."

"We ain't about to give you no trouble," Anse said as he obeyed, and Drew agreed as he followed the Texan into hiding.

"I'd like a rifle jus' 'bout now," Anse remarked. "Only thing I've ever held 'gainst a six-gun is that it don't throw lead as far as a fella could sometimes want it to. But I think we've sorta been ruled outta this here fight—'less th' enemy gits close 'nough to spit at."

Now they could see down the cut of the pass. The narrow passage wound between rocks and Drew, though he could not spot them, did not doubt that Rennie's forces were snuggled in where a surprise volley could do the most good.

"Somethin' sure is comin'." Anse had one hand flat on the ground. "Feels like th' whole danged army hoofin' it an' fast!"

Drew was aware of it, too—the vibration carrying through stone and soil. The drumming of hoofs, horses coming at a run. Now it was more than vibration, a distinct roll of sound magnified and echoed. And he caught a shout or two, the cries of men hazing on laggers. It must be Kitchell on his way through to the border!

A dust haze, rising like smoke. Then the foremost runner of the band appeared in the cut, the whites of its eyes showing, patches of foam sticky on chest and shoulder. Five . . . ten . . . an even dozen—but not a gray coat among them. One light buckskin had almost startled Drew into rising until he caught a second and clearer look.

The leaders were through and a second wave was coming. Drew counted twenty more horses before the first rider appeared. His face was masked against the dust by a neckerchief drawn up to eye level. But, unlike the ordinary range rider, he wore an army forage cap in place of the wide-brimmed hat of the plains. As he spurred by below Drew's perch he glanced up but seemed to have no suspicion that he was under observation.

There came more horses, and Drew stopped counting. But the gray he sought was not among them. The shouts of the drivers were louder. And then, as three men appeared bunched, there was a crackle of shots. Two of the riders fell, one leaning slowly from the saddle, the other diving into the dust. The third tried to turn but did not get his horse around before a mule pushed into him, followed by another and another. The horse thieves were trapped. Drew could hear the sharp snap of shots along the pass. More than those three must have been caught in the ambush.

The mules, braying and running wild, thundered on south after the horses. Then a saddled horse, riderless, galloped by with a second at its heels. Confused shouting rang out, without any meaningful words. This was as much a muddle, Drew thought, as any battle. You never saw any action except that immediately about you—mostly you were too busy trying to keep alive to care about incidentals. Come to think of it, this was about the first time he had ever sat out a fight, watching it as a spectator.

The roll of firing was dying down. Anse grinned at him.

"Takes you right back, don't it now?" he asked when he could be heard. "Th' Old Man, he's got him some of th' Gineral's idears—work good, too!"

"I didn't see Shiloh in that band." Drew stood up. "Couple of duns . . . no grays."

"Come to think of it," Anse agreed, "that's right! But lookit that bay down there." He pointed to one of the saddled horses that had a dragging rein caught in a dead juniper stump and was trying to pull loose. "Got th' RR brand! Some of these must be from th' Range raid."

"Hey—down here—!" The hail broke down the pass from the north. Rennie climbed over his rock barricade, and other men came out of cover to move up the cut. Since no one tried to stop them, Drew and Anse went along.

"Got us two of 'em ready to talk!" Jared Nye strode to meet his employer. "They're Kitchell's gang, all right. Only he ain't with 'em."

"*Patrón*—" For the first time since he had known him Drew saw Bartolomé Rivas run. He was weaving in and out among the fallen men in the pass. "They ride." He was half choked by the effort to force his message past heavy gulps for breath.

"Who rides?" Rennie demanded.

"Three—four men . . . that way." He waved a plump hand to the east. "They go like the wind, *Don* Cazar. And one—he rides the big gray!"

Drew whirled. The big gray—there was only one horse to be named so on the Range. Some of the outlaws had escaped the trap and one was riding Shiloh! Drew found the horse with the tangled rein, jerked and tore at the leather strap, and was in the saddle when a hand caught at the rein he had just freed.

"Where do you think you're going?" Hunt Rennie demanded.

Drew snapped the rein out from the other's hold. There was only one thing he wanted now, and that was getting farther and farther away with every second he wasted here.

"After Shiloh!" He used spurs on the horse and it leaped ahead. For all he knew any one of the posse might take a shot at him, so he rode low in the saddle. He heard startled cries, saw Bartolomé Rivas stumble as he got out of the path of the wild horse. There were rocks, sand, a body which the horse avoided in a leap, then there was free ground and Drew settled down to ride.

A horse was coming up from behind—they need not think they were going to stop him now. Drew turned his head as the mount pulled level with his own. He was ready to fight if need be. Only the man in the saddle was Hunt Rennie.

"Better find out which way to go before you break your neck or that bay's legs," Rennie called. "Out beyond that pillar—then east."

Drew nodded. But Rennie did not fall back. He was riding his heavy duty horse, a grulla famous for its staying power. And now the Kentuckian regained his proper share of common sense and began to pull in the bay. As his father had pointed out, a broken neck or a horse's broken leg was not going to bring Shiloh any closer. He heard the sound of other horses and glanced back as they wheeled around the pillar to the east.

Four riders were bunched—Anse, Nye, Teodoro, and Donally. That made six of them in all, pursuing four fugitives over miles of countryside which might have been shaped with no other purpose in mind than to shelter men on the run. But perhaps they could come up with the quarry soon. . . .

Shiloh! He had to get Shiloh! Drew began to call upon all the horseman's knowledge and scout's lore that he possessed. Those qualities, rather than fighting power, were what he believed he needed now. With luck—always with a large-sized helping of luck!

16 ❋

"Now that you have that bucked out, how about a little sound reasoning?" Hunt Rennie still held his position, riding stirrup to stirrup with Drew.

The worst of it was, *Don* Cazar was right. This was no time for raw emotion to replace thinking. Already it was almost dusk and their quarry could not be traced into the dark, even if they had the aid of a full moon. The Kentuckian reined in. Growing shadows masked the country ahead—rough territory—which he did not doubt the fugitives knew far better than he did.

"All right." It was difficult, one of the most difficult things he had ever done, to admit even that much that he must follow Rennie's lead. "What do I do now?"

"You still think you can go it alone—want to?" Rennie's face was shadowed, and his voice again held that remote note.

"It's my horse." Drew was defensive.

"Stolen on my range," Rennie retorted. "This is far more my fight than yours. If we didn't get Kitchell back there at the pass, and I'm inclined to believe that we did not, then I want him! You don't kill a rattler by cutting off his rattles—you go for the head. But this rattler's on his home land and he knows where to hole up. We have only one card to play against him."

"What's that, suh?"

"Water. Oh, I know all the rumors that the Apaches have secret water holes back in the hills, and they may have introduced Kitchell to some of them. But the hills are behind him. He'll want just one thing now, to get south, across the border. He's lost a large number of his men, probably all of his loot, back there at the pass. He can't hold out here any longer. Once he's into Sonora we can't touch him—I know he has friends down there."

"Could he try to take the wagon road south?"

"As a last resort, perhaps. The pass was the only outlet through which he could run that band of stolen horses and his pack mules. But there are other places, at least two I know of, where a few men, riding light, can get through. I believe he'll try to head for one of those."

"Make it ahead of us now?"

Rennie laughed shortly. "If he does, he'll have a warm reception. The Pimas are already scouting both passes. We planned to close the border when we set up that ambush. Meanwhile"—he glanced back—"Teodoro!"

"*Sí, Don* Cazar?"

"How far are we from your hunting-camp site?"

"Two, maybe three miles. Slow riding in the dark, *Don* Cazar."

"We'll head there. That—except for the hole behind us which Bartolomé will cover—is the only water for miles. And we're between Kitchell and the border spring. One thing he will have to have is water. We stake out the pools and sooner or later they will come to us."

It made sense, but still Drew was impatient. Out there one of Kitchell's men, or perhaps the outlaw himself, was riding Shiloh. The fact that Rennie's plan seemed a gamble did not make it any easier to follow. But the Kentuckian could think of nothing better to offer.

The moon was rising as they came to the water hole near the mustangers' camp. Men and animals drank together, and when Drew dismounted his weariness hit—hard. Fatigue was a gray cloud in his brain, a weight on arms, legs, body. Voices around him sounded faint and far away as he steadied himself with a grasp on the stirrup leathers and fought not only to keep on his feet but awake.

"What's the matter with you, boy?"

Drew tried to lift his head, tried to summon words to answer that demand. A sullen kind of pride made him release his hold and stand away from the bay, only to reel back and bring up hard against a rock, grating his arm painfully. He clung there for a moment and got out:

"Nothing a little sleep won't cure." He spoke into the dark outline of Hunt Rennie. "I'm all right."

Drew made a painful effort, pulled himself away from the rock to fumble at the cinches of the bay's saddle, only to be pushed aside.

"Steer him over there, Perse . . . bed him down."

The Kentuckian's last scrap of protest leaked away. He hardly knew when a blanket was pulled up over him as he lay in a rock niche, already drifting into deep sleep.

Voices awoke him into the gray of early morning. The light was hardly brighter than moonlight but he could make out Hunt Rennie, sitting cross-legged, rifle to hand, while Chino Herrera squatted on his heels before him. Chino had not been with them when they left the pass. And there was Greyfeather, too. Their party had had reinforcements. Drew pushed away the blanket and sat up, realizing he was stiff with cold. Fire . . . hot coffee . . . there was no sign of either. He yawned and jerked his coat straight about him. His attention suddenly focused on an object which lay on the ground at Chino's left. It was a book, the same size as the three he had bought at Stein's!

Without thinking, Drew moved forward, was about to reach for the volume when he heard the click of a cocked Colt. A hand swept down on the book.

"You, hombre—what do you want with this?" Herrera, with no friendliness in either voice or eyes, was holding a gun on him.

"That book—it looks like the ones I bought in town." Drew was startled by the vaquero's enmity.

"Give it to him," Rennie ordered.

For a moment Herrera seemed on the point of open dispute, then he obeyed. But for some reason his weapon remained unholstered. Drew took up the volume.

"History of the Conquest of Peru," he read out. The binding was a match for that of the other three. But—there *was* something different. He weighed the volume in his hand. That was it! This book was heavier. . . .

"Well, hombre, you have seen such a one before?"

"Yes, this is bound to match those I bought from Stein. And one of those was *History of the Conquest of Mexico.* This is surely a part of the same library."

"Those—what did they have in them?"

Rennie appeared content to let Chino ask the questions, but he continued to watch Drew and the book.

"Have in them?" Drew repeated. "Why pages. They were books to read—*The Three Musketeers, The Count of Monte Cristo,* and *History of the Conquest of Mexico.* That's all, just books."

"Open this one," Rennie told him.

The Kentuckian had trouble obeying. And for the first time he saw he did not hold a book composed of pages but a type of box. The cover resisted his tugging. Then, as if some catch had been mastered, it opened so suddenly he almost lost his grip on the book. The core of those once separate pages had been hollowed out to contain a nest of raw cotton on which lay . . . The Kentuckian gasped.

Even in this subdued light those stones glittered, and their settings were gold and silver. Drew saw elaborate pieces, the like of which he had never seen before.

"There was a mule shot back in the pass," Rennie explained. "His pack was opened. Three books were in it— one of them fell out and burst open."

"This one?"

"No, it held gold coin. *Hard Times* by Charles Dickens— the contents hardly indicative of the subject, were they? Upon investigation a *Wonders of the World* produced more coin. And, as you see, *History of the Conquest of Peru* was even more fruitful. You are sure this binding matches that of the books you bought?"

"Certain. This was bound to order, as were the other three. They were part of someone's personal library—had no bookplate, though."

"And what was Stein's story concerning them?"

"An old prospector named Lutterfield found them in a trunk in some cave he located out in the desert country. He brought them in to trade for supplies."

"Lutterfield," Rennie repeated thoughtfully. "Yes, that could be."

"Trunk in a cave?" Herrera was skeptical. "But why leave books in a trunk in a cave?"

"One of Kitchell's caches? Or else left by someone who cleared out in '61 and had to travel light. If anything remains, perhaps Lutterfield can locate it for us later. Anyway this"—Rennie took the book box from Drew, clapped the cover over, hiding the treasure—"won't go to Mexico now. And if the owner is still alive, we may even find him—who knows? You had your sleep out, boy?"

Drew found Rennie's expression one of indifference. Maybe *Don* Cazar no longer regarded him with the cold dislike Drew had met at the camp, but they were still strangers. What he had once said back in Kentucky at a remote and distant time was very true now. "Maybe Hunt Rennie doesn't know I exist; maybe we won't even like each other if and when we do meet . . . I don't know. . . ."

Now Drew thought he did know. Was this insurmountable barrier all his fault? Because he had been so sure he wanted to go it on his own—come to his father as an equal and not a beggar? But could he ever have acted differently? Too independent, too defensive always—Alexander Mattock had made him like that. Now it seemed that his grandfather had won, after all. Because his grandson was the kind of man he was, there would be no meeting with Hunt Rennie to claim kinship, nothing more than what now existed.

"I'm all right." After too long a pause, Drew replied to his father's question. "Do we just keep on sittin' here?"

"If necessary, Chino, pass those supplies you brought in. We eat cold, at least for now."

"You look ready to up saddle 'n ride." Anse was waiting behind Drew's rock. His arm rested in a sling with a neat and reasonably clean bandage about his wound.

"How's that hole?" Drew asked with renewed concern.

"Nothin' much more'n a nick. Say, th' Old Man's like a real doc, ain't he? Carries doc's things in his saddlebags an' patched me up last night so I'm near as good as new. After I drunk th' wrinkles smooth outta my belly an' had me some shut-eye, why, I'm as right as four aces in any man's hand! 'Course I sure could do with some coffee—'bout strong 'nough to float a hoss shoe gentle like. But we ain't bendin' lip over that this sunup. Lordy, this jerky sure gives a man's chewers a workout!"

They chewed away at the dark sun-dried *carne* of the border country. There was about as much flavor in it as in a piece of wood, but it kept a man's insides busy and about half satisfied. And they did have water.

Drew looked out over the land about them. Rennie had their small force stationed to cover every approach to the water hole, and with the Pimas here too, Drew was sure that they would not be surprised. Would Kitchell follow the pattern Rennie expected—try to water here? And then strike for the south? With his men scattered, many killed or taken at the pass, he had very little choice.

For some reason the quartet of fugitives must have been trailing quite a distance behind the main band, and so had been warned in time by the gunfire. Was one of that four Shannon? And what would it mean to Rennie if Shannon did turn up now with Kitchell?

Drew jerked back against the boulder, reacting to a screech from somewhere out in that wild country—a fierce, mad sound which tore at the nerves. He had heard its like before, but never rising so to the pitch of raw intensity. It was the challenge of a fighting stallion, one of the most terrifying sounds ever to break from the throat of an animal.

From the pocket meadow came the answering squeals of their own mounts, the pounding of hoofs as they fought their stake ropes.

"Don Cazar!" It was Teodoro. "The Pinto comes—and would fight!"

Again that shriek of rage and utter defiance. The rocks echoed it eerily, and Drew found it hard to judge either distance or direction. The wind was rising, too, scooping up dust to throw against men and boulders. But that wild stud could not be too far away, and what had stirred him to this point of vocal outburst?

"Teodoro," Rennie called, "get back there and see if you can quiet those horses."

Drew reached for the carbine he had taken from the boot on the saddle of the captured bay. Army issue . . . Spencer. He appraised it with the sharp, quick scrutiny of a man who had had to depend on enemy weapons before. Just how had this fallen into outlaw hands? The arm was well kept, ready for action.

Horses turned mean, turned man-killer at times. And the Pinto was reputed to be a murderer of his own species. Not just content to protect his band from a raiding stallion, he actually went out of his way to seek and force a fight with other males. Could it be that now the wild killer had been drawn from hiding to meet a strange stallion?

And could that stranger be Shiloh? It would mean the men they sought were circling back to this water hole. Shiloh and the Pinto! Even when saddled and ridden, the Kentucky stallion might respond to the challenge. And so handicapped he would have no chance! Drew bit hard on his underlip.

The yap-yap of a coyote sounded brazenly from the ridge behind which Drew was almost certain the Pinto had trumpeted.

"Pass the word," said Rennie. "Riders coming."

Anse hissed it on to Donally, who hid in the brush behind. Drew lay tense, as if his whole body was able to listen and assess sounds.

Waiting, as always, fretted the nerves. Imagination gave birth to sounds, made the quiver of a bush unnatural, planted in a man a growing sense of eyes boring down on his body, nakedly visible to the enemy. Drew's muscles ached. He forced tight rein on his imagination and began the hard task of consciously schooling himself past the danger of a freeze when and if attack did come.

Wind moaning about the rocks, sand blown in eyes and face. Twice Drew half put out his hand to the canteen which lay between him and Anse. Both times he did not complete the reach. His tongue felt swollen, the saliva in his mouth sticky, sickly tasting.

No sun—this was going to be a cloudy, overcast day.

He half arose. That scream came again, this time closer, more rage-filled. Drew turned his head.

"Cover me!" He did not give Anse a chance to protest.

That slope . . . he had been studying it carefully for long moments of the wait, gauging the distances between bits of cover, the tricky open spaces he would have to cross. But the riders they had been alerted to expect were not in sight, and if what he truly believed was about to happen did, the outlaws might never reach the water hole at all.

He was running, dodging, working his way up to the

crown of the ridge. But he was still too low to see what was going on at the far side when that scream of challenge was answered. The answer was deeper in tone, but it carried with it the same rising note of anger and fighting promise. Although Drew had never seen Shiloh prepare to give battle, he was sure he had just heard him voice such readiness.

The Kentuckian flung himself flat before he reached the skyline, wriggling on in a desperate crawl. Then he lay panting in a small earth dip, only a ragged fringe of grass between him and the down slope.

Even in the swirl of wind-blown dust there was no mistaking Shiloh—rearing and fighting to dislodge his rider, wheeling about in a circle. Three other horses and their riders had edged well beyond the circumference of that circle, the horses neighing and snorting.

The squeal of the Pinto was ear-wrenching, though as yet the killer stud had not appeared in plain sight. The cry triggered Shiloh into a fantastic effort. He reared, striking out with front hoofs, perhaps in an effort to keep his balance. Drew fully expected to see him crash over and back.

Apparently his rider feared the same fall. In the dusty murk the man separated from the horse. Shiloh whirled and pounded back, away from his rider, and as he went he voiced once more his answer to the Pinto.

Drew sighted a dark spot moving in to intercept the gray. Then the spot turned broadside and he appreciated what had made the Pinto so elusive to hunters. The mottled red-and-white patches of the wild stud's coat melted into the landscape in an uncanny fashion, making the horse seem to appear and disappear as he trotted back and forth.

The Kentuckian tried to bring the Spencer in line with that weaving, distorted barrel of spotted body. What was the range? Too far, he was afraid, for a shot to count. But he knew that he could not lie there and watch the Pinto cut down Shiloh in one of those vicious, deadly, equine duels. The Kentucky horse had no fighting experience, and his greater bulk and height would mean little against the wily cunning of the murderer who had already tasted blood too many times. To allow Shiloh to be ripped to pieces was utterly unthinkable.

The men down there no longer mattered. Drew rose to one knee, steadied the carbine, and fired.

Did the Pinto really flinch from a bullet striking home? Or had the dangerous sound of gunfire caused his old caution to win out for an instant over his blood lust? The red head with the dangling white forelock tossed, and then the wild horse whirled and ran. Shiloh, teeth bared, ready and willing to come to battle, followed. . . .

Drew was on his feet. Then he was pulled backward by a jerk out of nowhere, and he fell under a brown, mostly bare body which pinned him firmly to the ground.

17 ✻

DREW STRUGGLED WILDLY but he could not break the grip which held him down. He was looking up into the face of Greyfeather, and none of his writhing made any impression on the Pima's hold. There was a sprinkle of shots; then a whirl of the wind brought sand up over them, blinding eyes, filling mouth and nose. Even the Indian flinched from that and Drew managed to tear loose. He rolled down the grade, bringing up against a small tree with a jolt which drove most of the air from his laboring lungs.

He pulled his arm up across his face, trying to shield his eyes from the blast which thickened steadily, gasping for air to breathe. And the wind voiced a howl which arose as alarmingly as the stallions' screaming.

Stallions! Drew clawed his way up to his knees. But there was no seeing through that murk to where Shiloh had been. Then he was on his feet, stumbling along . . . the big gray must be hidden somewhere. . . .

"Drew!" A figure blundered into him from behind, almost sending him to the ground again. "Get down, you fool!" Hands clutched at his body, trying to pull him earthward.

"Let me go! Shiloh—"

"Get down!" Anse's whole weight struck him, and he fell, the Texan sprawling with him. It was only then that he heard the spatter of rifle fire and understood that they were in the middle of an exchange of lead slugs.

"Keep down!" Anse, his voice ragged with anger, snapped the command in Drew's ear. "What in thunder you tryin' to do? You gone completely loco, *amigo?* Walkin' right out to git yourself shot like them bullets was nothin' but pecans or somethin' like!"

For the first time Drew realized what he had done—blown Rennie's carefully planned trap sky-high. His shot at the Pinto must have been warning enough for the fugitives. But why were they trying to make a fight of it now, when to cut and run would have been the smartest move? Unless, having seen only one man, they believed he was alone. He tried to rub the dust from his eyes and think coherently. But all that was in the forefront of his mind was that last sight of Shiloh following the Pinto to battle.

"All right." Drew shifted in Anse's hold. "It's all right."

Not that it was, but at least that was the best way he could express his return to reason. And the Texan appeared to understand, for his grip loosened.

The dust which had blown up an opaque curtain dropped as quickly. They lay together on the far side of the ridge, but the space below was empty. They saw no men, no battling horses—nothing.

"They've hightailed it," someone called from the crest of the ridge.

"I tell you . . . I got one of 'em. . . . He's over between those two bushes. He'd pulled up to take up th' fella runnin' an' went out of th' saddle. Other man got his hoss an' lit out."

Drew stood up.

"Where you goin' now?" Anse demanded.

"Where d' you think?" the Kentuckian asked dully. "After Shiloh."

He went on foot, down the slope, across the open where the gray had unseated his rider and turned to take up the Pinto's challenge. Since the horses were no longer in sight, there was only one way they could have gone—to the east.

Drew was in the open when another of those wild sand and dust flurries caught him. Buffeted here and there, staggering, his arm up over his face, he was driven by its force until he brought up against a rock wall. With that as a guide he kept on stubbornly, because once more he had heard the scream of the Pinto. In triumph? Drew shivered under a thrust of fear which left him sick. He was sure that that murderous red-and-white devil had finished off Shiloh.

Along the wall . . . keep going. . . . The dust was thinning again. Drew's hand was on the Colt Topham had supplied. The Spencer lay back on the ridge. But if any kind of fortune favored him now, he was going to shoot the Pinto—if it was the last thing he ever did.

There was a clear space ahead once more. The sullen gray sky gave only dulled light, but enough to see by.

Drew had heard many stories of the fury of the stallion battle, and he had seen fearsome scars ridging the hides of two of the Range studs. But actually witnessing such a battle shook him. Teeth . . . hoofs . . . blood on Shiloh's shoulders and flanks . . . a strip of flesh dangling. . . . But Drew saw that the Pinto was marked, too.

The wild horse was trying for a final throat grip, and

Shiloh was on the defensive, running, wheeling to kick, once getting home on the Pinto's ribs so that the spotted horse squealed with pain. Shiloh had a torn ear and a gash open on his neck. The two battlers twisted and turned in a mad fury of movement.

Drew edged on, Colt ready. But to fire now was impossible.

The Pinto's hoofs crashed against the saddle and Shiloh gave ground. With a scream of triumph the wild one's head snaked out, teeth ready to set on the larger horse's throat. Hopelessly, Drew shot—it was all he could do.

The white-and-red head tossed. Shiloh had wrenched back. The Pinto drove against the gray and crashed down. It lay kicking as the larger horse hit out with forefeet, bringing them heavily down on the Pinto. The Pinto let out a cry of rage and pain that seemed to startle even Shiloh. The gray backed away from his writhing enemy and stood shivering, his head outstretched, nostrils distended. Drew fired for the second time and the helpless kicking was stilled.

Shiloh moved, limping. Blood matted with dust stained his coat, making him almost as red and white as the Range stud. Drew holstered the Colt and went to his horse, crooning softly as he caught one of the chewed and broken reins.

He was trying to examine what seemed to him terrible wounds, when Shiloh started neighing. The Kentuckian looked back. Anse and Rennie, with Teodoro and Chino bringing up the rear, were coming. The young mustanger went to look down at the Pinto.

"He is dead." That was an observation rather than a question. Teodoro knelt in the dust, drew his knife and cut loose strands of the long mane hair.

"I shot him." Drew was more intent on Shiloh's wounds. "He was killin' Shiloh."

He pushed back the thought that although his horse was still on its feet, the Pinto might have killed him, after all. Except for horses ripped by shellfire in battle, Drew had never seen any wounds such as these. He was deadly afraid that those two bullets had not really saved the stud.

"Let's have a look, Chino, bring my saddlebags!" Hunt Rennie was beside Drew. "Can you lead him back to the water hole?" he asked. "See if he'll walk."

Somehow they did it—Drew and Anse, Rennie and Teodoro. They coaxed, led, supported Shiloh when they could, and brought him to the water hole. And then they worked to stop the weakening flow of blood. Drew kept the young horse quiet while Rennie stitched up the worst of the tears.

"He'll do." Rennie washed his hands. "Can't move him for some time, though. He must have given a good account of himself meeting that murderer for the first time. Lucky . . ."

"Suh—" Drew found it difficult to face Rennie. As his anxiety over the horse's condition had faded, he had had time to think of something beyond his own affairs. "I want to say thanks." He got that out in a rush before he added the admission he must make: "I spoiled your plan to take Kitchell."

Rennie's dark eyes held his as they had always been able to do. Then Drew had the odd sensation that the two of them were all alone in a place not bound by space or time.

"Don't say you're sorry. If you did, I wouldn't believe you. You made the move you had to. If it had been Oro out there—I would have done the same."

Drew responded to that impulsively. "You're generous, suh."

His father's black brows drew together in a slight frown. "Generous? No, that's the truth. As for losing Kitchell— we may not have. Those who got away have Greyfeather, Nye, and others on their trail. And I do not think they will find such hunters easy to fool. Also, we have a prisoner. . . ."

Don Cazar's acceptance of their failure was so placid that Drew was led to make a wild guess.

"Not Kitchell himself!"

Rennie smiled. "No, we weren't that lucky—*you* must have had the lion's share of that commodity here today. We have a Mexican, name unknown. He was shot down while trying to pick up the rider Shiloh got rid of—who just might have been Kitchell. But this prisoner may be moved to tell us about the three who got away. If these wind storms keep up, they could powder over the trail and the boys will need help."

The Mexican, his shoulder bandaged, was propped up against the saddle they had taken from Shiloh. He stared at them sullenly, his gaze finally centering on *Don* Cazar when they took places opposite him.

"Some of that coffee for him, Chino," Rennie called. Herrera brought over a tin cup from the fire now blazing. As the Mexican took it awkwardly with his left hand, still watching Rennie glassily over the brim, the latter used fluent Spanish, only a word or two of which Drew understood.

The man grunted and then was assailed by Chino in a hotter flow of his native tongue, until Rennie silenced the vaquero's outburst with a wave of hand and spoke again.

Drew sniffed the aroma of the bacon Donally was frying, his stomach protesting plaintively.

"What are they sayin'?" he whispered to Anse.

"Old Man pointed out nice an' plain what th' Mex's in for, lessen he speaks up. This hombre, Rennie thinks maybe he don't run regular with Kitchell—more'n likely he came up from th' south, could be to guide th' gang back there some place. Iffen th' Mex can prove that, th' Old Man promises to talk for him with th' law. So far he ain't said nothin' much in answer."

They ate. The prisoner's round face expressed surprise when Rennie had him provided with an equal share. He sucked his greasy fingers avidly after he had wolfed down his portion. A moment later he asked a question of his own. Rennie replied, nodding vigorously, as if to make assent more emphatic. Anse translated.

"Th' Mex wanted to know if th' Old Man meant what he said 'bout talkin' up to th' law. If so, he may loosen his jaw some. I'd say, if he's a guide from down there, he wouldn't be too set on coverin' for Kitchell—not when that might mean gettin' his own neck stretched. Yeah . . . now he's beginnin' to run right over at th' lip."

The prisoner did loose a flood of words, Rennie and Chino listening intently, Donally coming to stand behind the others. Drew guessed by his changing expressions that the Anglo rider was as much at home in Spanish as Anse. The Kentuckian regretted his own ignorance; the few words he had picked up along the trail from Texas certainly were no help now.

The Mexican wiped his good hand up and down the front of his worn jacket, and then smoothed a patch of soil. On it he drew lines and explained each of them, much as Hilario Trinfan had done for the horse hunters days earlier.

"What's he sayin' now?" Drew demanded of Anse.

"That it's true he was sent to guide Kitchell south. That train of hosses an' loot was th' gang's prime pickin's. Some of it was to grease their way in with this hombre's *patrón*— don't know who *he* is—some Mex gineral or such. Kitchell, he rode behind because he had waited for a gringo to meet him. They was makin' up time when they heard th' fight goin' on in th' pass. Kitchell headed back here to fill canteens. Th' Mex was goin' to guide 'em south by another trail—one he knows. He's layin' it out for th' Old Man now. It's a pretty rough one; they'd have to take it slow. Could be we could catch up before Kitchell makes it—'specially since he don't have this Mex leadin' him now."

When it was necessary Rennie could move fast. He was on his feet giving orders almost before Anse had finished the translation. Their party was to be split in two. Drew and Anse were to stay with the wounded Mexican and Shiloh, and prepare to defend the water hole if the outlaws made a second attempt to come in. The rest of them would ride for an already designated rendezvous point where they would meet the party sent to trace the fugitives.

"Why do I stay, suh?" Anse protested when *Don* Cazar had finished.

"You can tend that arm better on the ground than in the saddle."

"Ain't no hurt there any more." Anse hurriedly pulled it from the sling. "Anyways, that ain't m' shootin' hand, neither!" But one look at Hunt Rennie's face reduced him to muttering.

Drew watched their preparations quietly. Then he

gathered up two canteens and filled them at the water hole, went back to loop their carry straps over Hunt Rennie's saddle horn. Anse had a bad arm, so it was right that he should not go chasing hell-for-leather over rough country. But Drew Rennie—he was left because he was useless in another way. He was a man who could not be depended upon, who had sprung their trap because he cared more for a horse than he did for the success of Rennie's mission.

And in a way Hunt Rennie was perfectly just in that judgment. If it were all to do over again, Drew knew he would make exactly the same choice. Shiloh was his—about the only good thing he had ever possessed, or might ever have in the future. If, in order to keep Shiloh, he had to give up what he knew now was a very vague dream—he would surrender the dream every time.

Although he knew that was the truth, the Kentuckian was desperately unhappy as he made a lengthy business of adjusting the canteens. About the worst words one could ever speak, or think, were "too late." This was all too late—twenty years too late. They might have had something good together, he and Hunt Rennie. Now it was too late.

As Drew heard the crunch of boots on gravel close behind him, he swung around. "Full canteens," he blurted out. And then, ashamed of his own confusion, he forced himself to look straight at his father. "Good luck, suh."

"We'll need it. I'm leaving you José—he'll do some prowling. Wouldn't do for you to be jumped by Apaches. If we don't come back in three or four days and Shiloh's able to travel, you take the Mexican and head back to the Stronghold—understand? I mean that."

"Yes, suh." Drew had lost his right to protest, lost it the instant he had betrayed their ambush. Now he turned quickly and hurried to where Shiloh stood. The last thing he wanted to see was Hunt Rennie ride away.

Anse kicked earth over the fire when they were gone. "No use showin' smoke," he remarked, and Drew readily agreed. The horses, with the exception of Shiloh, were hobbled and allowed the restricted freedom of the pocket-sized meadow running back from the water hole. Anse and Drew divided the night into two-hour watches.

"Don't see as how they'd be fool enough to try chewin' back on their trail again, though," Anse commented.

"They need water. Accordin' to what this guide of theirs says, they'll need it doubly bad before they finish that road of his. They might just be crazy enough to try here—men have gotten away with tricks such as that before."

"Drew." Anse was only a shadow among shadows, a voice out of the dark now. "You made up your mind about what you're goin' to do when this is all over?"

"Pull out—California maybe. I don't know."

"Sure you don't want to stay?"

"No!" Drew put explosive emphasis into his reply.

"A man can be too stubborn an' stiff-necked for his own good—"

"A man has to do what he has to," Drew snapped. "I'm turnin' in. Give me th' nudge when it's time."

He rolled in a blanket, settled himself with his Colt close to hand, and lay gazing up into the cloudy sky. What was the matter with him, anyway? All he had to do was stick to his decision. And that *was* the best one for him. Resolutely he closed his eyes and tried to will his mind a blank, himself into slumber.

"Drew—!"

Before his eyes were fairly open his hand was reaching

for the Colt, only to meet a numbing blow on the wrist. The Kentuckian rolled in instinctive reaction and a second, body-jarring stroke caught him in the ribs. He was left gasping, still not fully aware of what had happened.

"All right, you—on your feet!" A hand hooked in the collar of his coat to jerk him up. Somehow Drew did find his feet and stood bent over, his hands to his bruised side, breathing in small painful gasps. A rib had either been broken in that assault, or it was cracked.

There were two—three—four figures moving in the moonlight. Then the one fronting him turned and he saw the face clearly. Shannon!

"Only three of 'em—Benito an' these two," one of the others reported.

"How's Benito?" There was authority in that inquiry, but it came from the one man who kept well back in the shadows.

"Got him a holed shoulder."

"Able to ride?"

"Dunno, suh."

"He'd better be. We need him to find Graverro. These two we don't need."

"That's where you're wrong, Colonel. This here's about th' best cover we could git us now." Shannon laughed. "Mister Drew Rennie, come outta Kentucky to find his pa —touchin' story, ain't it? Real touchin'—like somethin' outta a book. Well, does his pa find us, his sonny boy'd be real handy, now wouldn't he?"

"You have a point, Shannon. We'll take him."

"An' th' other one, Colonel, suh?"

Kitchell—if Kitchell that shadow was—came out into the moonlight. He wore the gray shell jacket of a Confederate cavalryman, and the light glinted on the cords of a field officer's hat.

"Who are you, boy?" He faced to the left and Drew looked in the same direction.

Anse stood there, the barrel of a Colt pushed against him just above the belt line.

"Anson Kirby."

Shannon laughed again. " 'Nother big man—says he rode with General Forrest!"

"That true, Kirby, you were one of General Forrest's command?"

"It's true," Anse drawled. "Mean's nothin' now, th' war's long gone, hombre."

"Maybe it's over back east—not here! You stayed to the end, boy?"

"Yankees took me prisoner before that."

"Sergeant Wayne!"

"Yes, suh?" Anse's captor responded.

"Put him to sleep!"

18 ❈

DREW LUNGED and then reeled back as Shannon laid the barrel of his Colt alongside the Kentuckian's head. He was half dazed from the blow but he managed to get out his protest.

"You murderin' butcher!"

"Kirby ain't dead, he'll just have a sore head tomorrow," Kitchell returned, as the man he called Sergeant Wayne straightened up from the Texan's crumpled form. "And you—you keep a civil tongue in your head when addressing a superior officer. Shannon, no more of that!" The order stayed a second blow.

"Oughta shot him for real, suh."

"No. Not a man who rode with General Forrest." Kitchell hesitated and then added, "We'll be long gone before he wakes. Tie this one in the saddle if he can't hang on by himself. You may be right, Shannon, about him having his uses in the future."

"Say, Colonel, this here gray hoss, he's got hisself all hurted bad. Can't nohow go 'long with us. Want I should shoot 'im?" That whine came from the meadow where they had left the horses.

"No, leave him. Won't do Kirby any good and that's a fine horse—might just see him again some day. Sergeant, you fill all the canteens; take any supplies you find here. Then we'll move out."

Drew, his wrists corded to the saddle horn, both ankles lashed to the stirrups, swayed in the saddle as Shannon took the reins of his horse and led it along. The pain in his head and the agony in his side resulting from even the most shallow breaths, brought on a kind of red mist which shut off most of the surrounding night. He had no idea how the outlaws had managed to jump the camp. And who was the extra man with them now? Only three had escaped during the horse fight, but four rode in the present party. He could not think straight; it was all he could do to will himself to hold on and ride.

Drew was thirsty, so thirsty his tongue was a cottony mass in his mouth. The day was light and sunny now, and they were single-filing through a region of bright, colored rock wind-worn into pinnacles, spires, and mesas. There was no water, no green of living things—just rock and sun and the terrible need for a drink.

Maybe he moaned; Drew could not be sure. He saw the man riding ahead turn in the saddle. Blue eyes, the man had, with no honest life in them. Once before the Kentuckian had seen eyes such as those. It had been in a cabin—a cabin back in Tennessee in the dead of winter. A young bushwhacker wearing Union blue, with a murderer's eyes in his boyish face, had watched Drew with the same incurious glance which held nothing of humankind. Shannon; the bushwhacker—two of the same killer breed. But to recognize that no longer mattered. Nothing mattered save water. . . .

His mount stopped. Drew looked dully at the ground. Then his attention shifted to the man standing beside his horse.

"Down with you, fella."

Gray jacket, torn and threadbare—yet gray. Drew frowned.

"Sergeant Rennie, Buford's Scouts . . ." He tried to identify himself to this strange Confederate, but the words that got out were a thick mumble. Then, somehow he was on the ground and the man was holding a canteen to his mouth, dribbling blessed liquid over that choking cotton. Drew drank.

"Sergeant Rennie . . . must report . . . General Buford . . ." He was able to talk better now.

"Wot's that he's sayin'?"

"Somethin' 'bout some General Buford. Don't know who *he* is."

"Buford? Buford rode with Forrest." Those words were spoken by a different voice, sharper, better educated.

Drew opened his eyes, and for the first time actually saw the men he had been traveling with. The officer, who was maybe in his mid-thirties, had a beard trimmed to a point and eyes half sunk in his head. And Shannon—he had a half-grin on his lips as he stared down, enjoying what he saw when he surveyed Drew. The one Kitchell called Sergeant Wayne was a big fellow, even though he was thinned down. He had a square sort of face—jaw too heavy for the rest of it. Then, Drew's eyes came to the last man and stopped.

To the first three there was a uniformity; the remnants of military training still clung to them. But this shrunken figure with a wild gray beard, watery, bloodshot eyes, a matted thatch of hair on which a broken-rimmed hat perched, ragged and filthy clothing . . .

"Not gonna haul th' Mex much farther, you ain't!" observed this scarecrow with a touch of relish in the relaying of bad news. "He's outta his head now, gonna be clean outta his skin come sundown."

"All right!" said Kitchell. "We'll camp here . . . in that shade." His gesture indicated some point beyond Drew's range of vision.

"They're gonna be sniffin' 'long right behind us," the sergeant said dubiously.

"You're forgettin' we've got us sonny boy here!" Shannon loomed over Drew. "He'll buy us out."

"Maybe from Rennie—not from them Yankee troopers."

"I told you"—Shannon lost his grin—"th' Yanks ain't gonna come all th' way down here! There's too much pointin' in th' other direction. That is, if you was as good as you said you was, Lutterfield!"

The old man grinned in turn, widely set yellow tooth stubs showing ragged. "Ain't never failed you yet, boy. Old Amos Lutterfield, he's got him those wot believe wot he says like it was Holy Writ—he sure has! Them troopers'll go poundin' down th' Sonora road huntin' wot never was, till they drop men an' hosses all along. Then Nahata an' his bucks'll tickle 'em up a bit—an' they'll forgit there was anyone else t' hunt."

Drew lay in the position where they had dumped him, his hands still tied, the ropes on his ankles now knotted together. Had the season been high summer they would have baked in this rock slit, but it was still uncomfortably warm. He heard a low moaning and saw Kitchell and Lutterfield bending over the Mexican. It was plain that the wounded man had suffered from his enforced ride.

Some time later the Kentuckian was pulled into a sitting position. His hands loosened, he was allowed to feed himself, but the *carne* tasted like wood splinters when he chewed it.

"Not much like th' Range?" Shannon asked him. "Don't worry none—it won't last long, Rennie, no, it won't!"

"You did take my papers."

"I sure did! You thought I was clean outta m' senses back there in th' Jacks when that fool Texan called out your name—didn't you now? Well, I wasn't an' what he said sure made me want to know a little more—seein' as how Hunt Rennie might well be m' pa. He owed me a Pa, you know. M' real pa was killed gittin' him outta prison. I didn't want no drifters cuttin' in on what was rightly mine, in a manner of speakin'. So I just waited m' chance to get at that belt of yours. Found what I wanted—an' that sorta made up m' mind.

"Colonel Kitchell here, he wanted me to go south with him. They have them a war goin' on down there; a man can always git ahead in wartime does he like soldierin'. But I weren't sure 'bout goin', till I found out as how I might jus' be pushed out, anyway."

"Why did you think that? Hunt Rennie's always treated you as a real son, hasn't he?"

"Like a real son? Like *his* idea of a son, you mean. Work hard—an' havin' books pushed at me. Always jawin' about education an' bein' a gentleman! Do this, don't do that—this's right, that's wrong. Bein' soft with Injuns—Lord, I was sick of bein' his kind of son when I went off with Howard. Rennie wasn't even ready to fight th' war proper

—big man here, 'fraid to try it where he wasn't! Rightly he was sick of me, too, only his precious duty wouldn't let him say so.

"But as long as he didn't know 'bout you, he'd try, an' keep on tryin'. I had me a good place to hole up on th' Range. With you there he might'n't hold on to his patience. First off I thought I might settle you permanent, then you got took up by Bayliss." Shannon laughed. "That sure was a switch! Captain thought you was Kitchell's man, when he shoulda looked a little closer in a coupla other places."

"But you were shot—by Kitchell's men."

"I was creased by th' shotgun rider on th' stage we tried to stop. Boys brought me in close to town an' dumped me on th' road—gave us a chance to make up another tale to fool Bayliss. Me, I've been ridin' with Colonel Kitchell since '64. We come west from Kansas 'long th' end of that year. Th' Colonel, he saw what might be done out here where it's a long ride between sheriffs an' th' army hadda think 'bout Injuns most of th' time—what army there still was in th' territory. Me an' old man Lutterfield, we could help th' Colonel better not ridin' with him, but for him, as you might say."

"And now you're goin' to Mexico?"

"In time, Rennie, in time. Th' Colonel's thinkin' out some plans. *Don* Cazar, he was too lucky at th' pass."

"You're not goin' to get back those horses or mules—or what they were packin'," Drew said.

"We'll see, we'll see." Certainly Shannon's confidence was in nowise shaken. "Th' Colonel, he didn't want to call in Nahata an' his bucks—now maybe he'll have to. What we need is a lay-up till we can make some good plans. An' Benito, he'll arrange that."

"If he lives." Drew closed his eyes wearily. His face was one bruised ache where Shannon's blow had landed, and his side was constant pain.

"You'll see," Shannon promised. "We've got us a big ace in th' hole—th' Range boys don't know as how I'm with Kitchell, not yet. That's how we took you so easy back to th' water hole. I jus' rode up to José—got that there Pima listenin' to me till Lutterfield sneaked up an' put him outta business. Lutterfield, he don't look much, but he was runnin' in this country with th' Injuns thirty years ago. He's got th' Apaches lissenin' to him good. An' I can talk us through th' posses—maybe even into th' Stronghold later."

"You're a clever man, Shannon," Drew commented dryly.

"An' you're too free with that lip!" Drew's head rocked under a stinging slap which made fiery wheels of pain roll in his head. He must have been sent very close to the edge of unconsciousness for a moment or two.

"That's 'nough, Johnny," said Sergeant Wayne. "Th' Colonel says to keep him ready to move. You battin' him 'round like that don't do no good."

So Topham had been right—Johnny Shannon was Kitchell's man. Not that it mattered now. Even if, by some miracle, Drew could get away from this pack of wolves, he had no idea of where he was or which way to go. One man alone and lost in this country faced death as certain as the bullet Johnny Shannon had already loaded for him. There was only one thing—he was still alive, and as long as a man lived he had hope.

Nye and Greyfeather had trailed this bunch from the water hole. Perhaps the wind and sand storms had muddled the tracks, but Drew still had faith in the Pima. And Rennie's party had followed with the knowledge of the Mexi-

can's bolt hole to the south. Why, right now they could
have circled ahead—could be waiting for Kitchell again as
they had at the pass. An attack could give him a thin chance
of escape. He had best keep his mouth shut and not provoke
Shannon, maybe feign being more helpless than he was.

The outlaws had difficulty in getting the Mexican on his
horse when they were ready to move on in the evening.
Drew, seeing the man's swollen face, his half-closed, set eyes,
thought he was in high fever, probably no longer conscious.
Kitchell ought to have sense enough to know Benito might
not last out the night. But it was plain they were now
pushed for time.

They had been on the way for a while before Drew
noticed that Lutterfield was not with them. His reappear-
ance was far more dramatic than his going. A horse clat-
tered up from behind at a pace not in keeping with the
rough footing, and the rider drew level with Kitchell.

"Soldiers comin', Colonel. Got 'em a couple o' them
Pima Scouts sniffin' th' trail an' some o' Rennie's men with
'em, too!"

"It ain't true!" Shannon's protest was loud.

"I seed em—bright an' clear—mos' up to where we stopped
last. Iffen you wants to sit 'round waitin' for 'em, do it! I'm
clearin' out—ain't nobody can say Amos Lutterfield was
here."

"Nobody but us," Shannon said coldly.

"Lutterfield!"

Even Drew's head came around at that. The moonlight
was silver bright on the barrel of the Colt in Kitchell's grasp.
"Sergeant, suppose you take precautions to insure the continued company of this man. I don't intend, Lutterfield, to

let you curry favor by pointing out our trail to the army. I'd answer your proposed desertion as it deserves—with a bullet —but a body on our trail would provide an excellent signpost for any pursuers."

The rope which had been coiled on Wayne's saddle swung out in a perfect loop and tightened about Lutterfield, pinning his arms to his sides. His protests and roars of anger went unheeded and he rode on as much a prisoner as Drew.

"Move out." Kitchell motioned with the Colt. "Those two peaks ahead—according to Benito, the cut we want is between them. Across that we're free. The army can't follow us into Mexico."

But Kitchell still kept to a cautious pace. The risk of losing a mount was one he dared not run. Drew debated the idea of booting his own horse from their line of march and trying to ride for it. He need only hide out and wait for the troopers to pick him up. If he had had hands free and been able to move in the saddle to dodge bullets, he might have tried it.

The night wore on and Drew was driven to admiring the outlaws' nerve. Kitchell did not hurry; in fact he followed the old cavalry custom of resting mounts at regular intervals, seeing that each of the weary horses had nostrils and mouth wiped out with a dampened cloth. At the third halt he allowed them a drink of water before a smaller portion was given the men. Whatever else the outlaw might be, he was an experienced field commander.

They had the peaks looming above them when Benito gave a gurgling gasp and stiffened, tall in the saddle, before he looped into a limp, dangling bundle of a man. Kitchell called a halt. He dismounted to examine the Mexican before he beckoned to Wayne.

"He's dead. We'll need his horse. Put him down behind those rocks over there, Sergeant."

"You know where we're goin', suh?" Shannon asked.

"Enough to get us across the border. We can take cover there, make some other arrangements. Benito's *patrón* would not welcome us with empty pockets. Hurry, Sergeant!"

"I only got two hands, suh." Wayne had freed the body of the Mexican but was having trouble dragging it into the appointed hiding place.

"You help him, Shannon. We have no time to waste."

"What about him?" Shannon's thumb indicated Drew.

"I don't see how he can get away. Hurry up!"

Johnny dismounted with visible reluctance, but not before he blasted Drew's hopes by looping the reins of the captive's horse around his own saddle horn. And in addition Kitchell stood there with drawn gun. They had disposed of the body and Johnny was back when a sudden command boomed out of the air.

"Freeze!"

Shannon leaped, putting his horse between him and the open. He had the reins of Drew's mount in his hand. Kitchell went into a half crouch, and was startled into snapping a shot in the general direction of the voice.

Drew sat statue still. It was only too easy in this tricky light, bright though the moon was, to seem one of the men those ahead were hunting. He had no desire to stop a bullet now. But Johnny had ideas of his own. Under his direction Drew's horse broke to the left. There were shots and Drew flattened himself as best he could on the saddle horn, but not before he saw Kitchell spin around in a crazy dance and fall.

"All right, all right!" Shannon's voice was broken, ragged, almost as if he were sobbing. "You ain't got me yet—not by a sight, you ain't!" A knife flashed, cutting the ties which kept Drew's left boot to the stirrup. The Kentuckian was dragged down and held while the knife sliced again. Two more shots—then silence. Drew lay face to earth. The fall from the saddle had brought him down on his injured side, and he was in too great pain to take much interest in his surroundings.

Then he was dragged, pulled over on his back.

"I got Drew Rennie here." The call was one of desperation. "Yeah, hear that? Drew Rennie—th' Old Man's son. . . . I read them letters he had—it's th' truth! You come t' take me an' he gits a knife clean across his throat. I want me a hoss, water, an' an open road south. Do I git 'em—or does Mister High an' Mighty Rennie git him a son who ain't speakin' no more?"

"Johnny? Is that you, Johnny?"

"It sure is! Me, Johnny Shannon! An' I'm ridin' outta here free'n clear or else I'll do what I said. I mean that, Rennie! I surely do mean it. You lose me an' you git your real son—good bargain, ain't it?"

"You won't ride free for long, Johnny. You know that."

"I can have me a pretty good try, Rennie. This here's my country an' I know it well—better'n any but your men. Give me your word an' I'll go."

Drew tried to fight back the darkness which was closing in, a dark stronger than mere night shadows.

"Give him what he wants." The words echoed hollowly. Shannon drew a deep breath. He laughed softly. And

Drew made a great effort. He could see the bulk of the other's body poised between him and an opening between the rocks which must give on the pocket in which the outlaws had been surprised. Johnny was set like a runner ready on the mark.

The Kentuckian could hear the scrape of horses' hoofs on stone. They must be bringing out a mount, keeping Hunt's part of the bargain. Only, Drew suddenly knew, Johnny was going to keep him. He saw the gun hand shift against the rock—Johnny was taking aim into the pocket. Why? By trusting to Rennie's word he would have a slim chance, so why spoil it by some treachery?

"All right, Johnny, it's ready for you."

"Now you git them hands up, Rennie. Sorta guessed you'd come yourself. I'm gittin' out, all right. Do I take you along there ain't goin' to be no trailin', none 'tall—do they want *Don* Cazar to keep on breathing regular. Git them hands up, high!"

With all the force he could summon Drew kicked at Johnny's crouching body. Shannon cried out—there was a shot. Then Johnny cried again, this time with a choke cutting off the word as he arched convulsively against the boulder. In the half light the arrow projecting from between his shoulder blades stood out with unnatural clarity.

Arrow? Drew's wits worked slowly. The arrow must have come from one of the Pimas—Rennie had been covered, after all. So he had not believed too much in Johnny's promises. . . .

"You there, kid?" Someone came through the rock gap. "Hey—he's here all right, but he's hurt!" Nye's grasp on him brought the pain in Drew's side to an agony he could no longer stand. He was crushed down into darkness.

"Ribs are cracked, not broken—that's something to be thankful for. All right, you can let him down now. Give me that pad and some water; I want to see how much damage there is here."

Drew tried to turn his head away from the touch on his swollen cheek and jaw, but he was held steady to endure it.

"Best we can do for the present. You can leave the rest to me, Nye."

Drew opened his eyes. There was a fire near-by, but the flickering of the flames concealed more than they revealed of the face above him. He found the words to say rather than ask:

"You knew . . . before Johnny told . . . you knew. . . ."

"Teodoro told me—yesterday."

"I didn't lie. Johnny took the papers."

"He admitted it at the last. But why, why didn't you come to me?"

Put muddled feelings into words, attempt to explain what he did not fully understand himself? It was hard even to try, but you always faced up to the hard things.

"Wanted to know . . . if it was right . . . for both of us . . . had to know that."

"If you'd be welcome—that it? Well, what did you decide?"

What had he decided hours, days ago?

"Too late. . . ." But somehow that came out differently than he intended, as a question rather than a statement.

"No." The answer was uttered flatly, in a voice you did not argue with. "Suppose we begin all over again. You willing to try?"

"Better say—are *you,* suh?" Drew had whirling memories of all that had gone wrong since he had tried things his way. Then he saw a smile on his father's face, bringing him in—in where? To what? Suddenly he was eager to find out.

"Took the long way around to get home, didn't you?" Hunt Rennie asked softly. "I think we can make it worth the effort. Now, suppose you try some sleep—you've a pair of cracked ribs which'll have to be favored for a while. I think you've been too knocked about lately to make good sense. There'll be plenty of time."

Plenty of time. . . . Drew blinked. "Yes, suh." Obediently he shut his eyes. A blanket was pulled up, tucked in about him. For a moment a warm hand rested protectingly on his shoulder. And that reassuring pressure carried over with him into sleep, as if what he had long sought without recognizing was his, never to be lost again.